I0698797

WILLIAM BAER

Central Park

(A Romance in Central Park)

A Novel by William Baer

Copyright © 2024 by William Baer
Published by Winged Publications

Editor: Cynthia Hickey
Cover image: *New York Central Park at Night*
Bigstock

All rights reserved. No part of this publication may be reproduced, stored in a retrieval system, or transmitted in any form or by any means—electronic, mechanical, photocopying, recording, or otherwise—without the prior written permission of the publisher. The only exception is brief quotations in printed reviews. Piracy is illegal. Thank you for respecting the hard work of this author.

ISBN-13: 978-1-962168-74-8

*"This is a place to dream things
that never were – and ask why not."*

– Central Park Bench #00731

1. The Leap

Sunday, June 25th

I stood on the precipice, unaware of course that I was on the precipice of so much that would be totally inexplicable and incomprehensible.

Standing on the precipice of time itself.

I was wearing the same white dress that you saw earlier this evening at the screening. I was standing on a rocky promontory about twelve feet above the Lake, near Hernshead, and I was looking for little Jimmy.

It was early Sunday afternoon in Central Park, and we were playing hide-and-go-seek.

"Where are you?" I called out playfully. "I guess I can't find you. I guess I give up!"

It was a beautiful June day in the world's most beautiful park.

Idyllic. Perfect. Happy.

There was no response. Then I saw him, and my heart instantly compressed within my chest. Jimmy was sitting on a high branch in an old Elm tree, dangling over the waters of the Lake, waving and smiling.

"Be careful," I whispered to myself.

I did my best to try and remain calm, but I was terrified, with good reason.

Then it happened.

Jimmy slipped, lunged for another branch and missed, falling into the Lake. When he finally surfaced, he began thrashing in a terrible panic. I knew that he couldn't swim, and I knew that he was drowning.

"Help me!" I called out, uselessly.

But there was no one in sight. There was just me. Who like my little cousin had never learned to swim.

"Help me, dear Lord," I thought to myself, as if reflexively.

Then, oddly, I heard the chime of a distant church bell. It was 2:00. When it chimed a second time, I leapt off the precipice and everything went black, instantly, as I hit the water.

I have absolutely no recollection of the "blackness," but I assume that it was very much like death.

Eventually, I seemed to hear a young girl's voice.

"Are you all right?"

But I was still trapped within the blackness.

"Are you dead?"

I opened my eyes. I was confused and groggy. Discombobulated. I seemed to be lying on the shore of the Lake, in my soaking wet clothes, and I looked up into the pretty face of what, at the time, seemed like a little "immigrant" girl, who was, I would realize in time, just as American as me.

She was wearing a black t-shirt with "IF LOST RETURN TO THE CENTRAL PARK ZOO" printed in bold white letters across the front.

She smiled a lovely smile.

"You're beautiful," she said.

I had no idea what was happening, so I sat up and looked out at the Lake.

Then I remembered.

Horrified.

"Where's Jimmy?"

2. Softball

Thursday, June 18th

"You sure?'

"Yeah."

It was twilight in Central Park.

I was sitting on the visitor's bench, field #5 of the park's six Heckscher ballfields, eating Smarties, just as I always did on the bench. Three at a time. Let's face it, everybody's addicted to something, right? Well, I'm addicted to the little biconcave discs that they pump out across the river in Union, New Jersey. I once read somewhere that they've rolled-out over 2.5 billion Smarties a year, and I'd bet that I've eaten about half of them. Cherry, pineapple, grape, strawberry, and orange-cream. After all, who doesn't like yummy citric acid, dextrose, and calcium stearate?

I was wearing my button-up flannel baseball

shirt with "MIDTOWN NORTH" plastered across the front, and I had a bullet hole in my leg.

When I turned thirty a few months ago, I faced it "like a man," and I let the boys at the precinct sucker me into swatting around the "fatball." They all knew that I'd grown up playing a pretty slick third base, and that I was especially good at the plate, and that I always looked askance (not necessarily down) at softball. Sure, Eddie Feigner was superhuman. So was Jennie Finch. And I never missed tubing the NCAA women's college World Series.

But it was still "fatball."

Let's face it, hardball is hardball, and everything else is just an extrapolation.

"You think you can make it to first base?" Eric asked with appropriate sarcasm.

"That's assuming I can hit the damned thing first."

Despite all the kidding around, Eric was sweating it. He was a beat cop down in the theater district whose rep was always by-the-book.

"The chief would have my ass if he knew you were out here playing ball."

"I'm just pinch-hitting, Eric. Consider it part of my therapy."

He smiled.

Freddie was waiting on second, Reggie was

tagged at third, and Eric wanted to win really bad. We didn't actually hate the guys from Midtown South, some of whom were buds, but we hated their guts whenever we had to compete against them. Whether it was sports, collars, convictions, or anything else.

I stood up.

A week ago, a bullet had zapped through my upper-left calf. Just the muscle. No bone. It was what the movies like to call a "flesh wound," but whatever anybody likes to call it, it hurt like hell, but hopefully not so bad that I couldn't take a few cuts.

I walked over to the rack and picked up a 34-ouncer. I knew I had a slight limp, but it wasn't that bad.

When I got to the plate, Joey Esposito, who was catching for the Southies, seemed surprised to see me.

Even a bit concerned.

"You sure you should be doing this, Rick?"

"Let's find out."

The first pitch was high and inside. A fastball. I let it go.

The second pitch was another fastball, slightly outside, just below waist-high, and I plopped the fat stupid thing on a loopy rope into the gap in left-center. I wish I could say that I cracked the thing, but that's hardball talk, and this was "fatball." I hobbled down to first as Freddie and Reggie flew home. It was now: North 3, South 0, with one inning left, so Eric waved me back to the bench and sent in one of the rookies to pinch run.

My night was over.

Back at the bench, the boys said the usual good stuff, including Eric.

"Hell of a shot, Rick!"

And the usual wiseass stuff.

"It should've been a double!"

We all laughed, but it was perfectly obvious that Eric was already tasting his victory over the dreaded Southies.

"I think I'll reward myself," I said.

I strolled over to the concession stand not too far from Umpire Rock. I was feeling pretty good about myself. Maybe a lot of other stuff in my life was a mess right now, but I could still swing a baseball (softball) bat and help out my buddies.

The concession guy looked at me, ready to help.

"Give me a pretzel."

Another addiction.

"Yes, sir."

"You got a warm one?"

"Sure."

He nodded, then quickly produced from nowhere

a luscious, hot, fat, doughy, hyper-salty, NYC pretzel, but I was distracted, noticing something over by Umpire Rock. An older guy, seemingly all alone, suddenly vanished from my line of sight. As if he'd fallen. As if he'd had a stroke.

"I'll be right back."

As well as I could, I rushed over to Umpire Rock, and when I got there, the old man, maybe seventy or so, was lying on his back on the bedrock, and a young woman, wearing a CPMU (Central Park Medical Unit) shirt, was kneeling over him.

"What's going on?"

She was too busy to look up.

"Heart attack."

Reflexively, I pulled my cell and hit the button.

"Badge 6-2-5-0-5. We've got an apparent heart attack on the north side of Umpire Rock. We need an ambulance right away."

"He's not breathing."

She was calm, and she wasn't really speaking to me, but spoke as if she was talking to herself. Immediately, she began giving the old man mouth-to-mouth.

"Can I help?"

I didn't want to get in her way, but I'd handled plenty of emergencies on the Midtown streets.

"There he goes."

Again, as if to herself.

It was clear that the old man was breathing again.

She looked up into my eyes, and it blew the top of my head off. How can you describe such a thing without sounding familiar or derivative? Without clichés? Without saying it was "love" (or something like it) "at first sight"? Despite my initial exhilaration, my irresistible attraction, I wasn't perfectly happy about it given the situation, given the medical emergency.

Regardless, it seemed to me that she was having her own peculiar, maybe similar responses and apprehensions: shock-surprise, pleasure-elation, fear-terror.

All at once.

How could I possibly describe her? [Especially to Nikki who knows her so well.] Let me, rather unoriginally, point out that her eyes were greenish/hazel and oddly bright, as if ever-radiant, and that her hair was thick and dark with curls and whirls that fell down to her shoulders.

Instantly, I wanted to hold her, maybe forever, and I also wanted to kiss her lovely mouth, but I knew that I couldn't, and I knew that I shouldn't.

Then something else happened.

She looked down at the old man again and

quickly dropped her head down to his chest.

"Nothing."

Again, as if talking to herself, as if I wasn't even there. As if what had just happened between the two of us hadn't happened at all. She rose up on her knees and began striking his chest, then quickly leaning back down to listen to his inert heart.

Over and over.

I watched her uselessly, like a spectator, like a fool, noticing her name tag, "Alicia Appleton."

Finally, after many repeated attempts to revive the old guy, I wondered if it wasn't pointless.

"Maybe he's gone, Alicia."

She ignored me and kept at it.

"We'll bring him back!"

So I stood there watching her, fully expecting the worst, finally hearing the EMT sirens approaching from Central Park West. I wondered if I should somehow intervene. Maybe hold her arms, gently, and force her to accept what had just happened.

But I didn't.

Fortunately.

All of a suddenly, the old man startled a bit, and his eyes, full of fearful apprehension, popped open.

"You're going to be all right," she told him. "The ambulance is coming."

He seemed somewhat reassured, somewhat

comforted.

Alicia looked up at me again, confusedly, oddly.

"Are you a constable?"

Which sounded weird and peculiar, so she made an attempt to correct herself.

"Are you with Midtown North?"

Which I would have thought was pretty obvious, given that I was wearing a "Midtown North" softball shirt.

Before I could answer, she stood up and looked into my eyes. Once again. With the same exact effect.

"I have some blankets," she said, "I'll be right back."

Which didn't make much sense.

"But the ambulance should be here any minute," I pointed out.

But she ignored me, staring down at the old man.

"Stay with him, and wipe the foam from his mouth."

I did as I was told. I knelt down and held the guy's arm. There was, of course, no foam at his mouth. Or anywhere else. When I glanced behind me, I could see Alicia disappearing into the darkness beyond Umpire Rock, and I knew, without a doubt, that she wasn't coming back, with or without blankets.

I wanted to get up and go after her, even though I

knew I shouldn't, even though I knew she wanted to get away from me, even though the poor guy lying beneath me was fighting for his life.

"Don't worry," I assured him, "they'll be here soon."

I looked around me, high and low, finally seeing exactly what I wanted to see.

At the top of a nearby street lamp.

A surveillance camera.

3. The Cop

Thursday, June 18th

I looked up, and there you were.

You had no idea, of course, that I'd seen you before. On the day you were injured. On the day that you were shot by some kind of criminal. When I looked across the street, across Central Park West, and saw you for the first time. When, even from a distance, I felt compelled to be close to you, to go to you, to comfort you. Even though I had no idea why. Yes, you looked very handsome, strikingly handsome, even from a distance, even with the bright red blood soaking and dripping down the left leg of your pants.

Somewhere in the midst of all my confusions, I remembered that time when Nikki was watching Godfather III, which she said was "absolutely terrible," even though she'd watched it over and over again. Since I'm always wary of that kind of violence,

I was off reading one of my books in the Arsenal somewhere, and later, when I came back into the room where Nikki was watching the movie, I saw this amazingly, startlingly-handsome young man, with dark-black greased-back hair, intense deep-dark brown eyes, wearing a white dress shirt and an Italian suit, and I said "Who's that?"

Later, Nikki admitted that she had a "crush" on the guy, and that it was the real reason why she continued watching, over and over, a movie that she didn't even like, which she said was such a "crushing" disappointment after parts I and II.

"Andy Garcia."

She smiled.

"He proposed to me last week."

We laughed.

But I've never ever forgotten his face, or his name, as if the fates were telling me that it was impossible to forget such a thing, that it was, in some way, essential to my very being, my life, my life history, and so, when I saw you being helped into the ambulance on Central Park West up near 68th, I thought to myself, in the midst of all my swirling baffled illogical thoughts, this guy looks a lot like that mobster guy in the movie, but he seems to be some kind of cop, maybe some kind of detective.

There, that's the best I can do!

You looked like a young Andy Garcia.

(Even though I thought you were even more marvelous.)

So that night in the park, when I looked up (and there you were), my heart did some kind of weird imploding fibrillation, seeming to literally jump within my chest, and then immediately after its leap, it just lay there, uselessly, as if in shock, crushed with longing, crushed with love, which, of course, made absolutely no sense at all, especially to someone like me, who was always so rational, so practical, so wary of engagement, so wary of romance of any kind.

With good reason.

I was truly terrified by everything that I was feeling in my heart, the irresistible attraction, the overwhelming longing, and all the rest of it. It also seemed so terribly unkind, so terribly cruel, as if fate, as if time, which had already been abusing me for so many years, had suddenly brought you into my life at exactly the worst possible moment, being, as it were, a final coup de grâce, a final insult, a final debilitating cruelty.

All I could do was run away.

Like a frightened child.

<u>4. Zoo</u>

Friday, June 19th

"How many of you have heard the expression, 'See no evil, hear no evil, speak no evil'?"

She was standing on a small, outdoor, wooden stage at the center of the Central Park Zoo, babbling on about her stupid monkeys. She was wearing a zoo staff uniform, and she seemed to be about twenty or twenty-one, maybe Puerto Rican, with a cute face and frizzy black hair. Looking, I suppose, a little bit like J.Lo, back when J.Lo was still a teenager, before all the glitz, glamour, and makeup.

Immediately, all the delighted children raised their hands, as well as a few of their parents and other adults.

Everyone seemed to be having a good time.

Except me.

"Very good," she said, obviously pleased.

"Many people believe that the expression came from our wonderful Snow Monkeys from faraway Japan."

Behind her, on the screen, her video presentation had ended with a freeze-frame of a bunch of weird-looking creatures lounging around in a Nagano hot spring.

"Any other questions?"

An eager hand popped up. It was a little girl, maybe seven or eight.

Very serious.

"Do they really like to live in the snow?"

"That's a very good question! As we saw in the film, they mostly live in the forests in faraway Japan, but they can also live in very cold temperatures. They even like to roll snowballs for fun!"

This seemed to charm everyone.

Except, of course, me.

I'd spent the entire morning and all of the early afternoon talking to everyone who worked in the park – gardeners, custodians, concessions, maintenance, clerks, etc. – and every single one of them denied knowing, or even having heard of, someone named "Alicia Appleton." But I wasn't buying any of it. They were all lying. A cop can tell. But I couldn't very well cuff-em and run-em down to 54th Street, could I?

Since I couldn't grill-em, since I couldn't sweatem, I just kept moving.

The only people who didn't lie to me were the cops at Central Park Precinct on 86th Street, many of whom were baseball/softball buddies. They told me about an ICE agent who'd been looking for "someone like that," so I tracked the jerk down. He'd been on her case, "along with a billion other sketchies," for the past two years, after her identity had been exposed as fraudulent, and it seemed to him that she was probably illegal.

She didn't look like an illegal alien to me.

"If you see her, give me a call."

He handed me his card. His name was Bryan Murdock. Oops, let's make that "Special Agent" Bryan Murdock, a bigger-than-six-foot, thinks-he's-a-tough-guy Irishman with reddish-brown hair.

"Sure," I lied.

Then I headed over to the zoo and learned much-too-much about Macaca fuscata.

"Just remember," little J.Lo droned on, "what we all learned earlier: Macaque Monkeys are very very smart, and whenever it gets too cold, they like to warm themselves in the hot springs."

She gestured at the ridiculous picture behind her of about twenty-five of the fuzzy, furry, little monsters all huddled together within a steaming mist at the hot springs.

"Guess what?" she continued, "Those hot springs are actually heated by a volcano!"

Which seemed to impress everyone.

Whatever.

At least, it was finally over.

"Now, if you'll all go inside the habitat, you can see the monkeys themselves! But I do have an event-reminder for the adults in the audience. Tonight at 7:00, the park continues its Dress-Up Movie Series with a screening of *The Maltese Falcon*. Then, next Wednesday night, we'll be showing *Meet Me in St. Louis*. Thank you all for coming this afternoon! To the Central Park Zoo!"

The kids and the rest of the crowd applauded, rose from their seats, then headed off to see the bloody monkeys.

I walked to the stage.

"I've got a question."

J.Lo was collecting her papers at the podium. She turned around with a big smile, eager to talk about her creepy primates.

"Where can I find Alicia Appleton?"

"Who?"

She wasn't a particularly good liar. Her name tag said, "Nikki Cabrera."

"You heard me. I'm looking for Alicia Appleton."

She gave an unconvincing shrug.

"Never heard of her."

"You're lying."

"And you're very rude."

"Only when people lie to me."

Then it seemed to me that she figured something out.

She was a smart one. Definitely

I was wearing my typical off-duty stuff: black jeans, dark button-down dress shirt (today being hunter green), and my black "Members Only" windbreaker, which was unzipped.

The monkey-girl reached out and gently moved the front of my windbreaker away, seeing exactly what she expected to see, my shoulder holster and Glock 21.

I tried another tack.

"Don't worry, it's not official business."

She looked at me intently, unimpressed.

"It's none of my business at all."

Then she turned around and walked away.

I have to admit, I liked her self-assuredness. Her confidence. On the other hand, she definitely knew what I wanted to know, and she'd, rather coolly, put me off.

Let's face it, no one likes to be put off.

Especially me.

<u>5. The Pursuit</u>

Friday, June 19th

They told me, of course, that you were "coming," that you were coming after me, searching assiduously across the entire swath of the huge park. 843 acres. Pursuing me, relentlessly, across the margents of my world, across the margents of Central Park. Maybe even, I suppose, like those bloody Redcoats had once pursued George Washington, not far from here, when he was heading towards Harlem Heights with his decimated, undisciplined, colonial troops after the complete disaster at Brooklyn Heights.

Naturally, I was terrified, even though a part of me wanted you to find me, even though the sensible logical part of me did not. After all, it was all wrong, totally wrong, and the timing was off. It couldn't be *worse, in fact. After all, you can't pursue what really isn't there, or what won't really be there if you find it.*

    Who are you anyway?

    And why won't you leave me alone?

6. Surveillance

Friday, June 19th

"My girlfriend says they're childish."

I was standing in the ranger's little tech room, completely surrounded by baseball bobbleheads, maybe a hundred or so, all of them Yankees.

The ranger who was helping me was a guy named Eddie Mendosa. He was wearing a parkie uniform and sitting in front of a large computer screen scanning through last night's surveillance tapes. He was mid-twenties, put together pretty well, a likeable guy, and a bit of a chatterer.

I did my best to reassure him.

"I've got a room full of Hartland statues."

He was stunned. Amazed. Impressed.

Then he did exactly what I didn't want him to do, he stopped working, turned around in his chair, and looked at me with abject admiration.

"Whoa! For real?

"For real."

For the collectible-challenged, Hartland baseball statues are pretty much the gold standard in sports figurines. Back in 1958, somewhere in Wisconsin, the Hartland toy company started producing a line of baseball statuettes, eight-inches high, accurate, realistic, composed of acetate plastic, and painted with acetate-based paint.

"You got Mickey?"

Mickey Mantle was in the first batch they produced, soon followed by Willie Mays, Harmon Killebrew, Ernie Banks, etc. They originally sold for $1.98, were intended as a toy, but now, long after Hartland had gone out of business, they were still circulating for big bucks on the collectibles market.

"I've got them all."

I was simply stating a fact, not bragging, but I've never seen anyone so impressed in my entire life.

I guess for Eddie, it seemed impossible to believe.

"Every single one?"

"Yeah."

He thought it over.

"Wait until I tell my girl that I met a Midtown detective who collects baseball statues!"

I was glad I wouldn't be there for that

conversation.

Then I noticed a photo on the wall behind the computer screen, and I recognized the face.

"Tell me about her."

Eddie pointed at the photograph.

Proudly.

"That's her! Isn't she beautiful? The prettiest girl in Spanish Harlem! And the smartest too! She's been the absolute girl of my dreams ever since I met her five years ago, and I've proposed five times."

Which seemed to imply, at the very least, that four of them hadn't worked out.

Suddenly, there was a pall in the room.

"No luck?" I said delicately.

"Nope. None. She thinks I'm too, what she calls, 'complacent.' Too 'unambitious.'"

He made no attempt to dispute it, and now it was time for full disclosure.

"I guess I should have said," he admitted, "that she's the 'ex-girl' of my dreams. I was supposed to take the admissions test for the Police Academy this morning, but I chickened out. So I broke up with her instead."

I didn't quite follow his logic.

"Why'd you chicken out?"

He just shrugged. Since all of his revelations about his romance with the zoo-girl had led to a crash-and-burn, he turned back to his computer screen.

Work is always better than ruminating over one's broken heart.

"I'm almost there," he assured me.

Eddie was right.

Soon I was looking at the camera footage from last night at Umpire Rock. The images were pretty dark, and the three figures of interest were off a bit in the distance, but there we were: the old man lying on the bedrock, Alicia kneeling above him, and me standing there like an idiot, wishing I had some kind of purpose in life.

Alicia turned.

She looked up at me.

The moment.

"Freeze that."

Eddie did as he was told.

"You know that girl?" I said.

"No."

Unfortunately, even Eddie was a rather obvious liar.

"She's got a CPMU shirt on," I pointed out.

"Well, whoever she is, she doesn't work here in the park."

At least it seemed obvious that Eddie didn't enjoy lying.

Once again, it got me to wondering why everyone in the entire park would lie to an NYPD detective to protect this elusive girl. Why was she so special? What was going on? Did she have some kind of hold over them?

Or was it something else?

"Can you blow up her face and print it out?"

It wasn't a question.

"Sure."

"Make it as sharp as you can."

He got my drift.

The door to the little room opened behind me, and Eddie's boss walked in. I'd talked with the guy earlier this morning, and he seemed useless. He was somewhere in his mid-fifties, a bit excessive around the belt, and his name was Captain Keith Palmer. At the moment, he was accompanied by an elderly woman, maybe in her seventies, and she walked into the tiny room as, I imagined, she walked into every room, with supreme self-possession, regal bearing, and undeniable confidence. She also wore the kind of clothes that only rich people wear. Yeah, they kind-of look like everybody else's clothes, but there's definitely something different about them.

The price tag.

Naturally, I wished that she and Palmer would go away.

When Eddie realized it was his boss, he stood right up.

"Sir!"

Everyone ignored him, as the old woman walked over and stared at the face on the screen.

"That's her."

She looked at me.

"Where was that?"

Usually, I'm the one doing the interrogating, but I decided to play along.

"She saved a man's life at Umpire Rock last night."

The old woman thought it over.

"Who are you?" I said.

I wasn't rude, not really in-your-face, but Palmer jumped right in anyway.

"Miss Wellington's a park trustee."

He looked over at Miss Wellington, as if looking for her permission.

"If you don't mind me saying so, Ma'am," he continued, "she's a major donor to the park's Conservatory."

The old lady wasn't interested. She just stared intently at the image on Eddie's screen.

Then she spoke again.

Almost to herself.

"I've been looking for that girl for two years."

"Why?"

She was only partially evasive.

"When I saw the name 'Alice Appleton' in the Central Park Newsletter, I went to one of her lectures about the Shakespeare Garden, and I talked to her afterwards, but something was 'off.'"

Palmer decided to get helpful.

"We checked her out, and all of her IDs and references were fake, but she'd already quit her jobs at the park. Then she vanished."

"What jobs?"

"She worked with the gardening crew for a few years, and she also worked as a volunteer medic with the Medical Unit. Sometimes she'd give lectures in the park."

"About what?"

"Mostly about the park itself. The statues, the gardens, the history. Stuff like that. She's apparently an expert of some kind."

"Why didn't you tell me this stuff this morning?"

I knew why, of course, because the old lady was really the boss.

The captain shrugged, somewhat embarrassed, but the Wellington lady paid no attention.

"Why does ICE think she's illegal?" I asked Palmer.

"Because they don't know what else to think."

"What do *you* think?"

"I think she might be mentally unbalanced."

The old lady didn't like the sound of that, and neither did I, but when she didn't say a word, I continued.

"Why?"

"Because she behaves so weirdly. So erratically."

"Like what?"

He just shrugged, rather stupidly.

"Anything else?"

"Yeah, she's a ghost."

It seemed the best he could do, but Eddie couldn't resist butting in.

"Well, I think she's an angel."

The old lady put an end to her reverie and looked at me directly. It wasn't aggressive, just focused and curious.

"What's your department at Midtown, detective?"

"Domestic Violence."

Which didn't seem to make much sense.

"Then why are you looking for Alice?"

I looked her right in the eyes.

Did I mention she was wearing huge designer shades? Maybe Prada, maybe Dior. But I looked right in her eyes anyway.

"It's personal."
Now it was my turn.
"Why are you looking for her?"
She didn't miss a beat.
"It's personal."
I had to admit, I liked the old girl.

7. The Swimming Pool

Friday, June 19th

Later that night, I was swimming laps in the Lasker Pool at the north end of the park. I was getting stronger and stronger, as well as more and more determined. When I finished my final lap, I rested at the end of the pool, catching my breath, and I looked up at Nikki, who was sitting in her little lawn chair reading National Geographic.

"How was that?" I asked, looking for reassurance.

"You could swim the English Channel."

It wasn't really a compliment. When she threw me a towel, I got out of the pool and dried myself off.

I have two bathing suits, a red one and a yellow one, both admittedly old-fashioned. Tonight, I was wearing the red one. Personally, I like them both, but Nikki said I looked like something out of an Esther

Williams movie, which gives you some indication of how clever she can be.

"What's wrong, Nikki?"

It was a foolish question.

"How about June 25th. That's what's wrong! It's only six days away, and I'm sick about it. No, that's not correct, I'm much more than just sick about it, I'm terrified."

There wasn't much I could say, but I tried anyway.

"I know, Nikki, but we have to be strong. No matter what happens, we have to be strong."

"You've always been the strong one."

"That's not true. I don't believe that."

She shrugged her little Nikki shrug.

"And to make things worse, Eddie broke up with me this morning."

Which seemed perfectly ludicrous, almost laughable.

"What? Why?"

"He says I'm too good for him, that I deserve better."

I slipped into my terrycloth robe and sat down in the empty lawn chair, right next to Nikki.

"That just means he didn't take the police test this morning."

She knew it was true.

"Yeah, I guess so. I guess I'm feeling sorry for myself these days."

She smiled her little Nikki smile. The one that always lit up my totally-incomprehensible world.

"Besides, maybe he's right, maybe I do deserve better."

We both laughed.

She took my hand, and we looked at each other.

"What about you, Alice?" she asked. "Maybe it isn't so bad that some good-looking cop is searching all over the park for you. Maybe you should just let him find you? Why not?"

But we both knew "why not."

[Yes, my love, I fully realize that all of this is rather disjunctive, even rambling in parts, but I'm doing the best I can. Time's running out, and I'm writing all this stuff down, as quickly as I can, on top of Vista Rock, late Wednesday night, June 24th, since it's all that you'll have left of me tomorrow afternoon, and I want you to know what I've been going through. And what I've been feeling. And how I feel. And how I feel about you.]

Nikki looked up, and so did I, and we saw Eddie coming through the south gate. She wasn't pleased.

"Oh, hell, look who's coming."

She picked up her magazine again.

"I'm not talking to that idiot."

But truth-be-told, Eddie looked pretty sharp tonight. He was dressed in a rather authentic Sam Spade outfit, with appropriate fedora and a beige trench.

I tried to be nice.

"You look very nice tonight, Eddie."

"Thanks, Alice, but I really didn't enjoy the movie without you-know-who."

You-know-who was trying to pay absolutely no attention, reading assiduously about the predatory habits of the wild dogs of the Serengeti Plains.

"I thought you broke up with you-know-who?"

"I did. But I did it for her own good. Besides, I still asked her to go to the movies with me tonight, but she said that she'd never talk to me again."

She was doing a pretty good job right now.

"Well, Eddie, maybe you should let you-know-who decide what's best for her."

"Yeah, maybe you're right. Anyway, the real reason I came over here was to let you know that that detective who's trying to track you down now has a photo. He made me pull it off that surveillance cam at Umpire Rock."

Which was both concerning and confusing.

And flattering.

Eddie was still talking.

"Even though I'm not supposed to 'know.'"

"Know what?"

"That you're illegal, of course."

Which I guess I was.

Which I guess I am. In so many different ways. Being entirely displaced, undocumented, familyless, homeless, and all the rest of it.

"Thanks for letting me know, Eddie."

Eddie glanced down at Nikki, who seemed to be a million miles away. Then he slowly walked back to the gate and disappeared into the Loch, trailing his sorrows along the way.

"What an idiot!" Nikki decided, giving him no quarter.

"Oh, Nikki, he's just a big puppy dog. Besides, maybe I am an alien."

Which seemed to upset Nikki all over again. So she leaned over, and we hugged, with the same and only warmth that I'd ever felt since that fateful June 25th.

8. Alice in Wonderland

Saturday, June 20th

There.

I'd finally found her:

"Alice."

Wearing a short-sleeved light-blue dress, falling down to mid-calf, with old-fashioned puffed-out sleeves. With pretty white tights. With a lovely white pinafore, tied with a huge bow in the back. With cute, little, black ankle-strap Mary Janes on her feet. With a matching black hairband, tied in a tiny bow on top of her head.

The only difference that I could see, or remember, was the hair, being, today, not blonde like the Disney movie but her natural and very dark brown.

She was reading from the book with high drama,

theatrics, and mystery:

> *Alice opened the little box and found inside a very small cake, on which the words "EAT ME" were beautifully marked in currants.*

Her audience, probably about thirty little kids, was sitting on the grass at her feet, completely mesmerized, staring up at Alice/Alicia with something close to adoration, or at least infatuation.

> *"Well, I'll eat it!" said Alice. "If it makes me grow larger, I can reach the key; and if it makes me grow smaller, I'll creep under the doorway; so either way I'll get into the garden, and I don't care what happens!"*

The kids, with their parents and/or other accompanying adults sitting right behind them, sat there in the grass in a kind of hyper-ventilated anticipation, with all their, for the moment, angelic and adorable little faces completely wide-eyed before the amazing "Alice" standing in front of them.

> *So Alice ate a little bit, and she said anxiously to herself, "What will happen? What will happen?" And she placed her hand on top of*

her head to feel which way she was growing

. . .

Then Alice, like Alice, put her hand on top of her head.

. . . and she was very surprised to discover that she was exactly the same size! Now, of course, that's what usually happens when someone eats a piece of cake, but given all that had been happening, Alice was expecting only "out-of-the-way things" to happen, and it seemed quite dull and even stupid for life to go on in an ordinary kind of way.

Dramatic pause.

So she made up her mind, and she ate the entire rest of the cake!

Whoa!

What the hell would happen next?

Everyone waited with appropriately bated breath, whatever that means.

Then Alice looked down at all of her little children and closed the book.

"And that, my dear friends, is the end of the first

chapter of Mr. Carroll's *Alice in Wonderland*, called "Down the Rabbit Hole," and next week another volunteer will read you chapter two."

No one moved.

Which seemed virtually impossible because children in that age group, roughly seven to eleven, are always moving, twitching, locomoting, squirming.

Then it dawned on them.

It was over!

One of the little boys couldn't contain himself.

"But we want *you* to read it, Miss Alice."

The others agreed, with murmured consent.

Alice was visibly moved.

"I will if I can, Billy. I promise."

But another kid had no interest in waiting until next week to find out.

"Why can't we read more right now?"

Again, there was a categorical consensus.

"Oh, I wish we could, Thomas," Alice said, getting a bit mushy. "I'd love it too! Just like you. But your parents have other things to do today, and our time is up."

Then a sweet little girl, maybe seven or so, decided to speak for the masses.

"We love you, Miss Alice."

The others all concurred, and when it seemed as

though Alice might actually cry, things got a bit awkward for a few moments until one of the more perceptive parents started clapping politely, and everyone, young and old, joined in as well. Enthusiastically. Then the kids rose up, and like lemmings to the sea, swarmed the object of their affection (and mine). Holding her hands tightly, hugging at her hips with their faces pressed into her pristine pinafore, and all the other gooey little outward affections that emotional kids do when they want to somehow express what they're feeling inside.

It was, I suppose, it's fair to say, a rather bizarre scene. Disney's Alice standing in modern-day Central Park, after animatedly reading from *Wonderland*, being swarmed by a herd of emotionally-jacked munchkins.

Whatever I'd felt in my heart two nights ago when she looked at me near Umpire Rock was now stupendously conflagrated, and I wondered how-and-if I could, in some way, make this incredible young woman, whom I really knew-not-at-all, yet felt like I did, want me in the same way that I wanted her.

We were all, naturally and appropriately, on a stretch of grass near the famous Alice statue at the north end of Conservatory Pond in Central Park. I'd kept myself discretely hidden behind the eleven-foot-high bronze, which depicts Alice on top of a giant mushroom, surrounded by the Cheshire Cat, the White Rabbit, the Dormouse, the Mad Hatter, and me.

Eventually, sadly, the harsh realities of our non-Wonderland existence settled in, and all the hugging kids gradually found their adults, or vice-versa, and they wandered off in different directions into the rest of the park.

Eventually, I walked up to Alice/Alicia, not really knowing what to say, so I said something appropriately stupid.

"Is it 'Alice' or 'Alicia'?"

I guess I was kidding.

Then I realized that she was crying.

"Are you all right?" I asked, compounding my stupidity.

She lied.

"I'm OK. Fine."

She didn't seem surprised to see me. As if it was inevitable, like taxes, like death, like a death sentence.

I waited, and she tried to explain herself.

"I love these kids so much."

I got that.

"But why won't you be here next week?"

Which brought her back to reality, and she instantly turned the tables.

"Because people are chasing me everywhere I go."

She wasn't angry, or even accusatory, so I changed the subject. Rather dramatically.

"You look beautiful."

She didn't seem to mind at all, but she was worn-out emotionally, so she stepped over to the statue and sat down on a mushroom next to the Mad Hatter.

When she looked up into my eyes, I tried not to fall in.

"Why are you pursuing me?"

"You know exactly why I'm pursuing you."

She *did* know, so she looked away.

"You know what?" I said.

"What?"

"You're much more mysterious than Alice ever was. And a lot more suspicious."

But she was a bit suspicious herself.

"Have you read the book?"

"No," I confessed.

She looked at me like my teachers used to look at me whenever I'd revealed some kind of intellectual deficiency.

"But," I added foolishly, aware that it definitely wouldn't help, "I saw the movie."

"Of course, you did."

Which actually sounded less dismissive than it reads on the page.

Since I was already floundering, I floundered forward.

"My favorite part was when Bill got sneezed out of the chimney, and the Dodo says, 'There goes Bill!'"

She laughed.

You might remember that Bill was a green lizard with a Cockney accent whom the Dodo commandeers to remove the giant Alice from inside the house. When the Dodo pushes Bill down the chimney, the soot makes Alice sneeze, and Bill shoots up into the sky, never to be seen again.

But my "teacher" wasn't about to let me off with a laugh.

"It's different in the book."

I waited.

Nothing.

"How is it different?"

"Well, you'll just have to read the book, won't you?"

Since I had no response, I resorted to (what else?) flattery.

"You're a terrific reader."

It worked. She was flattered.

"I guess I've had lots of practice. I've often read

stories and fairy tales to my two little sisters. Like Hans Christian Andersen, or the Grimms, or Arabian Nights, or, sometimes, some of my own."

"How old are your sisters?"

"Twelve. They're twins."

She was starting to sound like a real person.

"Tell me one."

"What?"

"Tell me one of your stories."

She smiled, thought about it, and gave me a taste.

"Well, the girls always like the one about the pretty princess who's given a magical 'talking teddy bear,' who speaks in rhymes and helps her choose the right suitor."

"Was his name Teddy?"

"No," she smiled. "His name was Billy. Billy Bear."

"Would you tell it to me sometime?"

"Maybe."

She looked up at me, rather mischievously.

"If you behave yourself."

"Sure," I said, "I can do that."

"Good."

Then I did the exact opposite. I picked up her little white purse, took out her wallet, and checked her IDs.

"Can detectives do that?"

She wasn't really angry.

More playful.

More resigned.

"Only when people use false names and addresses. Or when they have fake IDs in their wallet."

She didn't bother to deny it.

"By the way, are you 'Alice' or 'Alicia'?"

"Alice."

I found a photo.

It was the only photograph in her wallet. An old black-and-white. The guy was definitely handsome, *too* handsome, and he was wearing an old-fashioned suit with a high collar.

"Who's this?"

I held up the picture.

"My boyfriend."

"I doubt that."

She seemed slightly offended.

"Look," I said, "we both know it's not true."

"And why is that, Mr. Snooping Detective?"

"Because it's a picture of Christy Mathewson, a Hall of Fame right-hander who won nearly 400 games, and who rather singlehandedly won the . . ."

"Stop!"

She was rather furiously waving her hands in

front of her face, as if to prevent me from talking, as if to prevent herself from hearing whatever she didn't want to hear. Then, just like a little girl, she put her hands over her ears.

"Don't tell me anything! Please, don't tell me anything else!"

I didn't know what to think.

"Why?"

She took her hands away from her ears.

"Let's just say that I have my reasons, and leave it at that."

"Fine."

The last thing I wanted to do was upset her.

Rather deftly, she shifted the subject.

"How come you're such a smarty-pants about baseball history?"

I told her the truth.

"I think it's fair to say that baseball saved my life when I was a kid. It kept me busy, and it kept me happy. And it kept my mind off my problems."

She seemed to understand.

"It's important to have something like that in your life."

"Is that what Central Park is for you?"

"I guess it is. I never thought about it like that before."

She stood up.

Which made me nervous.

"I need to stretch my legs."

"Fine, but I'm coming with you. You're not getting rid of me that easily."

She seemed pleased, and she smiled.

"All right, let's walk through the park."

"Good. You can tell me about yourself."

"Well, I'd prefer to tell you about something else. Like the park."

I decided not to press it.

At least for now.

"All right. Tell me three things about the park that I've never heard of."

She seemed to like the idea, as we started south, heading toward Conservatory Pond.

"Is your leg OK?"

I guess I was limping a bit, and she seemed concerned.

"Yeah, I'm fine. Some moron shot me through the leg last week."

She nodded, saying nothing, asking nothing.

"Tell me about the park."

We headed down the pathway toward the pond, which was perfectly lovely beneath the summer sun, dotted with many small white sails on the many small white sailboats.

As we made our way along, everyone who

passed by seemed perfectly pleased to see "Alice" from Wonderland strolling through the park in the middle of New York City.

As if it was nothing-but-normal.

My lesson began.

"All right, copper, I bet you didn't know that George Washington once retreated across the northern edge of the park after the Battle of Brooklyn Heights. Of course," she reminded me, "it wasn't a park back then."

So we talked a bit about Washington, Nathan Hale, Mad Anthony Wayne, and Major André, until she said, rather playfully and rather pleased:

"I didn't expect you to be so smart."

"I'm really not. But I do like history, and I do like baseball."

"Me too."

We cut back, heading toward the Hans Christian Andersen Statue.

"All right, here's some more park history. I bet you didn't know that there was once a big-time nightclub right here in Central Park."

I had no idea.

"It was called the Casino, and many of the biggest stars of the day performed in the ballroom. Eventually, however, it got a seedy reputation, and they ended up tearing it down in the Thirties."

I was thinking to myself that I'd like to take Alice to a "ballroom" some time. So we could dance. So I could hold her in my arms.

For now, we walked and talked together, down a tree-lined pathway near Pilgrim Hill, not quite arm-in-arm, but I believed, maybe too hopefully, heart-to-heart.

"All right, Miss Central Park, how about something romantic?"

She seemed to know just the right thing.

"There's a famous old love story from way back in 1905."

I waited.

"It happened during the Harlem championship football game when a young footballer named Morris Friedlander was running with the ball and accidentally crashed into a young woman named Bertha Persky."

"And they got married?"

She frowned playfully.

"You're worse than the children! Why can't you act like a big boy and just wait for the ending?"

"So they got married?" I repeated.

"Yes, they got married!" she agreed, with mock exasperation.

I was undaunted.

"I bet this park is *full* of love stories."

"Yes," she said thoughtfully. "Definitely."

By now, we'd looped all the way around Pilgrim Hill, crossed under Park Drive, and were approaching the eastern edge of the Lake, eventually wandering into the southern Ramble to The Point at the end of the peninsula. Pretty Bow Bridge was off to our right, the famous fountain was directly across the water, and the Boathouse was off to our left.

As with Conservatory Pond, there were numerous sailboats gliding across the water, and closer to shore, there was a dozen or so impervious white swans. We sat down on a white bench and watched the white sails and the white swans glide across the sun-glistened surface of the Lake, beneath a lush and deep-green canopy, surrounded by the beauty of everything at this ever-serene ever-beating "heart" of Central Park.

For a while, we just sat there in the silence, like lovers who'd been comfortable lovers for a long long time, who could take each other for granted for the rest of their lives, and certainly not like two never-really-met-before people who'd spent about fifty-five minutes together, and who knew absolutely nothing about each other.

Except that her name was Alice, and she had two sisters.

Finally, it was me who broke the silence.

"I think I'm in the middle of one of those Central Park love stories right now."

I said it as if I was kidding, but we both knew that I wasn't.

She didn't respond, so I tried to mollify.

"At least, I think I am."

Which gave her an "out."

But she didn't take it.

"That would be lovely," she said, not quite committing herself.

Then rather preposterously, yet rather appropriately, just as such things can happen in Central Park, we heard a lovely romantic song floating across the waters from the Boathouse.

She laughed.

"Now we've got the right kind of music!"

She looked at me, and she crushed my heart.

"It's so lovely. Do you know what it is?"

"It's a song called 'Could This Be Magic' by a group called The Dubs."

She seemed greatly affected.

The lyrics were simple enough, but the lead voice of Richard Blanton was, well, to be perfectly honest, "magical":

> *Could this be magic, my dear,*
> *My heart's all aglow;*

Could this be magic,
Loving you so?

"It's beautiful. What kind of music is it?"

"It's called Doo-Wop. It was very popular in the late Fifties."

She seemed surprised.

"Why do you know so much about it?"

I guess I hesitated.

"Tell me. Please."

So I did.

"When I was five years old, my parents died in a terrible car crash on the Bruckner Expressway, and I spent the next two years with my grandmother until she also died. Anyway, she played Doo-Wop music all the time, and I loved her very much, and it was a very important time in my life."

She was still curious.

"Then what happened, Rick?"

It was the first time that she'd said my name.

"I kicked around some foster homes for a while, both in the boroughs and over in Jersey. Some good ones and some not-so-good ones. Eventually, I ended up at a pretty good prep school in New Jersey, went to Rutgers, played baseball, and became a New York City cop. Just like my old man. Whom I can barely remember."

That was my entire life in a few sentences.

"It's not much of a story, Alice."

"Well, I think it is."

The Dubs were still singing across the Lake.

"Why don't we follow the music?" I suggested.

Since she seemed to like the idea, I stood up and held out my hand, and she held out hers, which was the first time that we touched, which would take a semi-literate cop like me more than quite a few hours to attempt to describe.

Inadequately.

Slowly, we made our roundabout way to the Boathouse.

Could this be magic, my dear,
Having your love?
If this is magic,
Then Magic is mine.
Could this be magic?
Then magic is mine.

When we arrived at the perimeter of the Boathouse patio, several nicely-dressed couples were dancing to "Tonite, Tonite," which had followed right after "Magic." When the song ended, the dance floor cleared, and the next song began.

One summer night, we fell in love.
One summer night, I held you tight,
You and I, under the moon of love,
moon of love.

"That's 'One Summer Night,'" I explained. "It was one of my grandmother's favorites. And one of mine."

I turned and looked at Alice, closely face to face.

"Let's dance."

She hesitated.

"Look, Wonderland, you've got two choices, either you dance with me right now, or I'm going to kiss you right on your pretty mouth."

She laughed.

"Well, that's a real Hobson's choice, both being a fate worse than death."

"You've got five seconds."

I was actually hoping for option two.

"OK, let's see if the cop can dance."

We stepped onto the dance floor, and she fell into my arms.

We fit together perfectly, as if ordained since Adam and Eve first bothered to take a look at each other.

Once again, I couldn't possibly describe what I was feeling and what I hoped that she was feeling.

Let's just say that it felt like I was holding my love in my arms.

It was slow, intimate, and ridiculously romantic.

> *One summer night, I kissed your lips.*
> *One summer night, I held you close,*
> *You and I, under the moon of love.*

It wasn't night yet, and there was no moon in the sky, and I, very foolishly, hadn't kissed her yet, but it was the most wonderful dance of my life. If a cop is allowed to use the silly word "wonderful."

Maybe I should take a break right-here-and-now and address the "mushiness" problem. How does a city cop with a billion busts, not to mention several billion DV (domestic violence) bust-ups, talk about something like love? Well, he doesn't. At least, not very well. But I suspect it's a bit like what Dr. Johnson said about the dancing bear. Don't expect it to dance very well, just marvel that it dances at all.

Maybe I should take this a step further:

Sure it's embarrassing to listen to a six-foot-one, one-hundred-and-ninety pound, afraid-of-nothing cop talking about mushy stuff, but let me quote some stupid poem that a buddy of mine, Eric Powers, the guy from the ballfield, showed me one time. He'd fallen, like a Mack-truck-full-of-bricks, for a pretty

Dominican girl, and he was constantly embarrassing himself around the precinct singing her praises. Naturally, he ended up taking a lot of abuse from the other guys, including me, who called him a wimp and a pussy, and a lot worse. Finally fed up, Eric stood on top of his desk, fully prepared, and read out loud, very loud, some dopey poem, which I guess is a sonnet, whatever that is, that he'd read in some equally embarrassing book of love poems. Which I didn't know anybody bothered to write anymore. He read the thing with astonishing conviction, and everybody listened. Even the chief came out. When it was all over, the boss said, "All right, ass****s, get back to work and leave poor pathetic lovestruck Powers alone." Then he looked at Eric, still standing on the top of his desk, and said, "By the way, I happened to enjoy it, Powers, but maybe you could put your jingles away for now and do some work."

Of course, if you're wondering, Eric eventually married the girl.

It was called "Sappy Love Poem":

> *The poets, who used to think otherwise,*
> *will read this sonnet, scoff and snipe,*
> *call it embarrassing, and roll their eyes*
> *at its mushy, low-brow, sentimental tripe.*
> *Well, the hell with them! What do I care?*

When you still "walk in beauty" every night,
the moonlight in your eyes and windswept hair,
the inexplicable "phantom" of my delight;
when you're the only thing I'm thinking of,
in the city, the bedroom, or on the beach,
where we've confabulated this hyper-love
with "two hearts beating each to each,"
whose hearts still jump when the other enters
    the room,
thump-thump-thump, and, yes, boom-boom-
    boom.

I bet the guy who wrote it, the "poet," must have been catching some abuse as well, so he basically said screw everyone and wrote his little in-your-face ditty, with its 'boom-boom-boom." The next day, after I'd admitted to Eric that, just like the chief, I kind of liked it, a hard copy appeared on my desk, without the name of the unknown bozo-poet, since it was probably stolen off the web. So now I've included it right here, as my own "what do I care if anybody thinks my feelings for you-know-who are a bit over-the-top, mushy, sloppy, and lovey-dovey."

When the music stopped, the dance was over, and I'd blown my chance to kiss the one I knew I loved. We walked over to a neat little isolated table at the edge of the dance floor, and I said my bit.

"Look, Alice, I don't care who you are, and I don't care what your name is, and I don't care how elusive you've been in the past. I'm a cop, and I'm never going to let you get away from me again. Do you understand that?"

Against her better judgment, she capitulated.

"Yes."

"Do you realize that I can find you anywhere? *Anywhere.* Right?"

She understood, and she nodded, and she accepted it. Then, with unexpected tenderness, (how else can I describe it?), she gently touched my face.

"You have no idea how foolish this is," she said.

"Why? Tell me."

She nodded again, resignedly.

"All right, I will."

Then she glanced over at the refreshment stand.

"But first, I'd like something to drink."

I stood up.

"All right, whatever you want."

Thinking wine or booze, or maybe even a Coke.

"Just water. With some ice, please."

I walked over to the Boathouse bar and looked back at Alice, who was looking exactly like Disney's Alice, looking perfectly spectacular, and, of course, I knew exactly what she was up to.

The bartender came over.

"What would you like?"

"A glass of water with some ice."

He dropped some cubes in a glass and poured in some bottled water, the kind that I never drink, preferring NYC tap water, and I gave the guy an over-the-top tip, and he thanked me.

When I turned around, Alice was gone.

Just as I'd expected.

"Damn it!"

I'm not sure why I said it, since I was fully expecting it, but I did anyway. I suppose that no guy with a bullet hole in his leg wants to chase Alice through her Wonderland.

I left the glass on the counter, stepped away, and caught a glimpse of a light-blue dress heading south toward Rumsey Playfield beneath East Drive.

I followed her.

Eventually, she turned toward Wisteria Pergola and cut across Bethesda Terrace.

She maintained a steady pace, never looking back, even though she surely knew that I was coming after her. Maybe she was expecting that my bum leg would give out, or maybe she had something else up her sleeve.

Which is exactly what worried me.

I lost sight of her near Cherry Hill, which really spooked me, so I headed up to higher ground and spotted her over by Navy Hill, not too far from Bow Bridge. If my leg didn't hurt so bad, I might have been able to see the humor in me relentlessly pursuing Alice, just like Alice had once relentlessly pursued the White Rabbit.

She swung over toward Bethesda Fountain, quickly heading north toward the Glade. I managed to keep her in sight the whole time, but then she suddenly did a one-eighty-turnaround not far from where we'd started earlier at Loeb Boathouse. Then she walked under the Trefoil Arch and vanished into the darkness within.

Worried, I quickly closed the gap and rushed beneath the arch. When I came out the other side, it was obvious that she was gone. Which seemed impossible. I went up to the top of the arch and scanned the entire area.

Nothing.

No Alice.

Not even a White Rabbit.

Everything was deserted, perfectly still, perfectly silent.

Irritated at myself, angry at myself, I went back to the north end of the arch and reentered the darkened tunnel, finding nothing that seemed suspicious. Frustrated, I clicked on my cell phone flashlight and carefully scanned the ceiling, the floor, and the surrounding walls.

Then I saw it.

A fairly large open drain on the eastside wall. The opening began at ground level and extended upwards for about four feet. Immediately, despite the rising discomfort in my left leg, I bent down and entered within a large stone drainage pipe. Using my flashlight, I moved, rather cautiously, through the old pipe, which was more like a creepy underground tunnel. After negotiating a particularly awkward bend in the tunnel, I saw the iron grating. It was old and rusted, but it was locked with a newish-looking key-lock. So I did what any idiot would do, especially one who'd just been duped by a girl wearing an Alice in Wonderland costume, I rattled the grating like a caged animal.

To no effect.

"Damn it!"

9. The Running Away

Saturday, June 20th

Why do we do it?

Why do we run away from what we really want?
Or what we believe we really want.

I suppose I had a better excuse than anyone else in a similar situation. Although I doubt that anyone in the entire history of the universe had ever been in such a situation before. I also wondered if it was possible that anyone else in the same entire historical span had ever felt the same kind of stupendous, irresistible, unearthly, and ultimately doomed attraction that I felt for my cop, for you, my darling, who collects baseball statues.

Maybe it's just vanity.

Maybe people fall in love like this all the time.

Of course, even calling it "love" seems perfectly ludicrous. I'd spent less than a few hours with

Richard "Rick" Kincaid, with you, and I knew next-to-nothing about you, and you knew less-than-nothing about me.

Yet somehow it didn't seem necessary to know anything at all, to know any kind of "this" or "that." Not once that I'd actually seen you, my love. Not once that I'd looked into your eyes. Not once that we'd danced in each other's arms, drenched within what, from my limited and inexperienced view of the world, could only be love.

Yes, I know it's all wrong. Completely.

I also know it's perfectly impossible.

Whether in your world, this world, or my world, which often seems so unworldly, so ephemeral, so permanently lost and inexplicable.

So why shouldn't I "try"?

Why shouldn't I give in? Why shouldn't I let you catch me, and hold me, and maybe even kiss me on the mouth?

Why do we, so often, run away from what we really want?

Were my excuses anymore justifiable than anyone else's?

I really don't know, but then I'd think ahead to June 25th, even though I was trying so hard not to, and I would run away.

What else could I do?

Yes, I knew that you were following me, patiently, relentlessly, despite your injury, just like a cop, close but not too close, just like a pursuing lover, and I could feel you behind me, feel your heat, your love, trying to catch me, trying to find out who I was, and where I came from, and where I lived, and all the rest of it, but I fled away from you like a child.

Who cried all that night on Vista Rock.

Feeling sorry for myself.

Feeling sorry for you.

Because I knew that you'd try and hunt me down forever, but I'd always escape.

Always.

Because nobody knows this park better than me.

Nobody.

10. Rooftop

Sunday, June 21st

I got a tip that Baaden was hanging in the park over near Strawberry Fields, but he saw me coming, and he ran like a madman across Central Park West, dodging traffic, ignoring the screeching brakes and blaring horns.

He always kept himself in pretty good shape. Soccer shape. He was a few years younger than me, twenty-sevenish, with a lean and hungry look, being, uniquely, half Dutch, half Dominican. Baaden was also very fast on his feet and given the fact that it was now post-soccer-time in the afternoon, and given all the morons he'd been hanging around with, I would have bet the ranch that he was also jacked on coke, which was always the creepiest thing about the guy.

"Coke" eyes.

Suddenly I was racing up the stairwell of some

upscale apartment building near 68th Street, and I knew, without a doubt, that the schmuck was headed for the roof. I think, in his heart, he realized that despite his coke-fueled athleticism, I was eventually going to run him down, so he took to the roof, like many of the pea-brains tend to do, hoping to lose their pursuers within the sunbaked labyrinths of the adjoining rooftops.

Three flights above me, I heard the door to the roof slam, and, in no time, I was blowing through the same doorway and racing along the tar-top at the top of the city, with the lush-green park down below me to my right. Maybe fifteen stories high. Even though I don't have a heights problem, which, after all, would be pretty much of a job-disqualifier for a city cop, I was never that comfortable chasing creeps from rooftop to rooftop, which was, of course, exactly what I was doing. Racing across the top of New York City after some coked-up cretan with a penchant for beating women to a pulp.

He fired his first shot.

He wasn't really aiming. He just lifted his arm behind him as he raced from roof to roof and started firing at random, hoping, I suppose, to slow me down.

To give me pause.

Which it didn't.

At the far edge of one of the buildings, he suddenly vanished. In an instant. Within a momentary moment. And I thought to myself how nice it would have been if he'd fallen down the fifteen flights, but I knew, of course, that it was actually just another "roof jump," which I hated, and this one was down about a half-story. So I took the leap, flying off the one roof, into the hot afternoon sky, as carefully as I could, trying to land as solidly as possible, trying to protect my ankles, onto the adjacent roof.

It worked.

I took the fall just fine, perfectly in fact, then continued racing after Baaden, without breaking stride, over a long stretch of level rooftops.

Intermittently, Baaden was firing backwards, without even looking, missing wildly, and I paid no attention.

Until I had to.

One of them, probably his fifth random shot, must have ricocheted off a metal chimney-vent, blowing itself through my left calf and out the other side.

I felt it, but I really didn't feel the pain, so I figured that I could just keep going. Then rather uncontrollably, I started slowing down, and I knew that the bastard was going to get away, so I pulled out my Glock, fired in the air, and called his name:

"Baaden!"

I wasn't that far behind him, and he didn't want to take a chance on getting shot in the leg from behind, so he stopped where he was and turned around.

It seemed as though he wasn't even out of breath.

It didn't matter.

I had him.

Then my leg buckled, and Baaden realized that I'd been hit, and he looked at the edge of the roof.

"Yeah," I said, "go ahead and jump."

So he did.

But not before he gave me his f-you smile.

After collapsing down to the floor of the roof, I started, rather pathetically, crawling across its warm tar surface toward the edge of the building, so I could see what had happened.

When I finally stuck my head over the edge, I could see that Baaden was heading down the fire escape, quickly, without, it seemed, a care in the world, as if he was on a carefree jaunt to meet his buddies at the poolhall, so I fired a second shot in the air, which got his attention.

He stopped where he was, about two stories below me, and he looked up.

He had the look on his face that every cop hates.

The I-know-you're-not-going-to-shoot-me look.

He was right. As much as I would have liked to make the world a better place, a Baadenless place, I wasn't about to shoot the bastard in cold blood.

So we stared at each other a bit, then he smiled his slimy smile and was just about to continue down the fire escape, when I unloaded my entire clip.

I'd seen the metal awning above him, and I noticed that its left-side bracket was old, rusted, and not-too-sturdy-looking, so I blew it apart and the whole thing crashed down on the top of Baaden's stupid head. As he fell in a heap, pretty much lifeless, onto the sun-hot metal of the old fire escape.

Which made me feel good.

Real good.

I have to admit, honestly, that it was like something (blowing away the bracket) that you might have seen in an old-time western movie.

I pulled out my cell, called it in, and woke up.

When I opened my eyes, I was looking at Willie Mays and feeling an attention-getting throb in my left leg. My Willie statue was standing on top of the bureau next to my bed, between Harmon Killebrew and Mickey Mantle. It was a pleasure to wake up every single morning in my big lonely bed and see the three "power" boys, who, in their day, had pounded the hardball with legendary ferocity.

I sat up in my bed, with my mind slowly clearing, ignoring my leg.

Two things amazed me.

One: that my dream was so amazingly accurate, being exactly what had happened on the city rooftops ten days ago.

Two: that for the first time in three days I didn't wake up thinking about Alice, although immediately I realized that I *was* thinking about Alice.

I suppose getting a .38 slug tunneled through your leg is about the only thing that could trump thinking about Alice in Wonderland. Thinking about love. At least, momentarily.

At least, when you're semi-unconscious and still half-asleep.

Forty-five minutes later, I was down at the precinct, sitting in the boss's office, waiting for the chief.

Deputy Inspector John Walker of Midtown North.

The room was exactly like the boss. Neat, uncluttered, with perfectly framed photos of his family, along with various other photos of himself with the people he respected, people like Mayor Giuliani and Commissioner Bratton.

Walker came through the door.

He was huge, tough, mid-fifties, likeable, and

competent. He was also one of the few cops on the force who still remembered my old man.

For the past eight years, he'd been my friend and mentor.

Ten days ago, he'd been forced to go to Chicago for some "stupid" chiefs' conference, and now, as was perfectly obvious, he was glad to be back at Midtown.

Back home.

I stood up, and we shook hands.

"You good?" he worried.

"Yeah, I'm fine."

He believed me, so we both sat down.

"What happened? I've heard bits and pieces."

I told him my dream, which was also the truth, as he listened carefully.

Then I wrapped things up.

"I called it in, the guys came, and they took me to St. Luke's."

He thought it over.

"Sounds like a lucky shot to me."

He was smiling.

"Which one?" I kidded. "His or mine?"

"Both."

Then he got more serious.

"Tell me about it."

Referring to the leg.

"It's a through-and-through. I'm fine."

He nodded.

"And Baaden?"

"Indestructible as always. He got knocked out briefly and took a few stitches in the top of his head. That was it."

"He's a lucky bastard."

The thought bothered me.

Quite a bit.

"Yeah, I should have shot the slimeball in the chest."

"That's not a good thing to say to your boss."

Of course, it wasn't.

I shrugged then tried something else.

"Well, at least, he's off the streets for now."

"Yeah, and you've got yourself a nice little vacation, right?"

He smiled again.

"What have you been doing with yourself?"

I told him the truth.

"I went over to the Jersey shore."

We both knew what that meant.

"Barnegat Light?"

"Yeah."

Which was where Heather had drowned.

Three days after they let me out of St. Luke's, I drove to Long Beach Island, crossed the causeway at

Ship Bottom, and headed north toward Old Barney. The island was still showing, three years later, the after-effects of Hurricane Sandy, when its eighteen-foot seas and nine-foot storm surge had pounded the crap out of the beautiful barrier island.

Not to mention the rest of the New Jersey Shore.

So I drove up to the old lighthouse, which, it seems, has now become not only the symbol of the New Jersey shore, but the symbol of the entire state, appearing on a few billion license plates, and I walked down to the water and sat down in the sand.

Like every Jersey guy, I love the ocean, and I love the shore, but I hate the sand. Sure, it's pretty and picturesque from a distance, but it's clingy and invasive up close.

At that moment, I didn't really care.

A year after the hurricane, while I was working at Midtown and chasing after the Baadens of the world, Heather was down the shore with her girlfriends from Morristown, jet-skiing off the Barnegat coast, doing what everyone in the state was supposed to be doing, "normalizing" after the Sandy trauma.

By all accounts, she was having a great time, when she accidentally brushed against another girl's jet ski, lost her balance, toppled, smashed the side of her head, went under the depthless Atlantic, and never surfaced again.

At least, not alive.

The girl I'd met at NYU, who was the girl I loved and planned to marry, the girl who said she loved me and who wanted to marry her "tough-boy cop" was suddenly dead.

A fluke accident.

Now two years later, I was still trying to deal with it.

I guess getting shot, even in such a fortunate flesh-wound-kind-of-way, had focused my mind.

After all, death is always sitting right across the room or lurking around the corner.

Or waiting in the chamber of a thirty-eight.

Or lurking in the cool waters off Barnegat Light.

So I sat in the warm stupid sand and stared out at the ocean and talked to Heather. Not out loud, I suppose, but I spoke to her just the same. Just like I always did, with love, with respect, with honesty, as I spoke my little mind and my little heart, and all that I got in return, the only answer I received, was the crashing of the waves on the shore in front of me.

Yet somehow, it was enough.

Maybe I didn't believe that I was ready to "move on," but I did believe that I was ready to try.

Three days later, some bogus medic in Central Park looked me in the eyes and rocked my little world like a billion Hurricane Sandys.

The chief tried to be delicate.

"Did it help?"

"Yeah. It helped a lot."

He seemed satisfied, so he left it right there, and he got back to business.

"When you coming back?"

"Next week."

He seemed to be waiting for some kind of explanation, so I gave him one.

"I met a girl at the ballfield the other night, and I'm tracking her down."

He laughed.

"Good. You could use a girlfriend!"

"But I've always got Helen."

Who was always a comfort.

An hour later, I was down in the tech room, sitting on the edge of Helen's desk. She was fifty-fiveish, a long-time widow with two well-adjusted, grown-up, and married daughters, and she always insisted on treating me like the son she'd never had.

Which I didn't mind at all.

She was also, without question, the best techie in the precinct, and she'd been doing some snooping around for her favorite cop.

"Sorry, hon, there's no such person. No 'Alice,' and no 'Alicia.' Although it looks like there was an

'Alice Appleton' way back at the beginning of the 20th Century. Maybe she lifted the name."

She looked at me directly.

"Is she pretty?"

I kidded her back.

"No, Helen, not in the least. You know that I prefer the un-pretty ones."

She looked at me as though I imagine a mother might look at her grown and lonely bachelor son.

"Well, you could use a girlfriend."

"Yeah, that's exactly what the chief said."

She was pleased with the corroboration.

Then she handed me a yellow post-it.

"Here's the other one. The zoo girl. Her name's Nicolasa Cabrera, and she lives on Lexington near 97th."

I looked down at the yellow post-it.

"The number on the top is her cell phone, and I want you to call her right now."

I hesitated.

"Right now."

Why not?

I punched in the numbers, and Nikki picked up.

She wasn't happy.

"I'm feeding the leopards. Why is Midtown bothering me again?"

"I'll feed you to the leopards if you don't give a

message to Alice Appleton."

"Alice?" she said sarcastically. "I've never known anyone named Alice."

I liked her spunk, but I ignored her.

"Tell her to meet me at 4:00 on Balcony Bridge."

"Anything else, copper?"

So I said it.

Why not?

"Yeah, tell her I love her."

Even over the phone, I could tell that the ever-unflappable Nikki was taken aback.

I hung up the phone, wondering if Alice might have been sitting there, right next to Nikki, listening to what I'd just said. Also wondering, whether she'd heard it or not, whether she'd show up at the bridge.

"Good job, Ricky."

Helen was the only person in the precinct who called me "Ricky," and I liked it, and I was glad she was pleased.

The captain came into the room, which he almost never did, so we knew something was up.

Something not good.

He didn't waste time.

"Baaden's made bail."

I was stunned, and more than a bit furious at whatever stupid judge had done whatever he'd done.

But I didn't say a word.

"I just found out, Rick. So he's back on the streets, and you need to be careful."

"Me?" I said dismissively. "What about Michelle?"

"I've already sent your buddy Powers over to her apartment."

The boss looked at me directly.

"I want you to keep out of it, Rick"

When I didn't say, "fat chance," or something similar, the cap repeated himself.

"I mean it, Rick."

I gave him a bit of a nod, and he left the room, probably knowing that he'd failed to do what he'd come down here to do.

Then Helen gave it a try.

"You should listen to him, Rick."

Yeah, she was right, but how many sons listen to their mothers?

For that matter, how many surrogate sons listen to their surrogate mothers?

"Give me Michelle's phone number," I said, "and I'll check her out by phone."

Which she really didn't believe, but she did it anyway, and she handed me another yellow post-it.

11. The Phone Call

Sunday, June 21st

Nikki was sliding the food tray into the feeding slot for the CP snow leopards, as the two young twins, Summit and River, lumbered over for their disgusting-looking lunch.

"Yummy," Nikki said.

"Yak," I said. "It's revolting!"

Nikki laughed.

"You don't even know what it is!"

"I don't want to know! Don't you tell me!"

In the meantime, River had started right in, but Summit, the ever-curious one, looked at me intensely with her weirdo pale gray-green eyes. It's true that mountain cats are very beautiful. No doubt about that. But they're also vicious killers, capable of bringing down prey over three times their size and three times their weight (meaning my size and my weight), capable of leaping over fifty feet horizontally, and capable, amazingly, of leaping over twenty feet vertically. Straight up into the air! Which was the reason for the extremely high fences around the snow leopards' compound in the middle of New York City.

Which provided minimal comfort.

Yes, they're beautiful, with their murky gray and blurred-black markings, their graceful movements, their weird three-foot tails. But they always give me the creeps.

But not Nikki. Never Nikki. She loved all of God's creatures, even the cold-blooded predators.

Finally, maybe concerned about getting her fair share of the meal, Summit looked away.

Which I much appreciated.

Then Nikki's cell phone went off.

To the salsa beat of La India's "El Hombre Perfecto."

When she checked her cell, she frowned her little Nikki frown.

"I'm not sure I like the look of this."

She sat down next to me.

"It's Midtown North. Probably you-know-who."

Then she smiled, got Nikki mischievous, and put her phone on speaker.

"I'm feeding the leopards. Why is Midtown

bothering me again?"

Then I heard your voice, and it made me feel nervous inside like a little girl, like a little girl waiting for her parents to take her to the circus, or a little girl waiting to open her birthday presents. Or something like that. Feeling almost out of control. At least, on the inside.

Of course, it was much much more than that. It was the thing that I'd read about in all the great books. In Shakespeare, in Austen, in the Brontës.

It was love.

It felt wonderful.

It felt terrifying.

So I sat there listening to your little back-and-forth with Nikki, each of you giving the other a hard time, and I thought of you holding me on the patio of the Boathouse, and I wanted you to hold me again.

"Anything else, copper?"

Then you said it.

You said:

"Yeah, tell her I love her."

I went completely strengthless inside, and I wanted to lie down on the bench and think about nothing else in this whole wide world. But, of course, I didn't. I didn't reveal a thing. Nothing.

You hung up at your end, and Nikki looked me in the eyes with her naughty adorable know-it-all smile.

"Wow, he's got it bad!"

She seemed truly amazed by your willingness to expose yourself. To confess how you felt inside.

By your bluntness.

I said nothing. Absolutely nothing.

I gave nothing away.

But, of course, no one knew me better than Nikki.

"Hey, wait a minute!" she realized. "So do you!"

She seemed excited by the possibility.

"Don't you dare deny it, Alice! I can tell. I can always tell what you're thinking. And you know that I can always tell!"

I shrugged, what else could I do, which was the same thing as saying, "Yes, you're right, Nikki, you're always right about whatever's going on inside of me, so, yes, you're absolutely right, I am, if it's truly possible, in love with somebody, some cop, that I barely know."

She mulled it over, but not too long.

"Well, it's about time!"

Meaning, of course, that it was about time that I was finally attracted to someone.

We both laughed.

Like little girls.

Then Nikki got Nikki-pensive, and whenever Nikki got Nikki-pensive, she also got dead serious, and you could almost hear the wheels turning.

"Why not, Alice? Why not meet with the guy?"

Then she did some evaluating:

"Besides, he's a looker. That's for sure."

"But what's the point?" I offered weakly.

But nothing could undermine her optimism, which was sometimes hopeful beyond all reasonable hope.

Hoping as much for herself as for you and me.

"Who knows, Alice? Maybe you've got it all wrong. Maybe June 25th won't be June 25th? Maybe nothing will happen. Maybe now you'll have something else to stay for?"

It was quite a lot of "maybes," and we both knew it.

Then Nikki leaned over and hugged me and kissed me, as she did so often, and I thought to myself how fortunate I was to have such a marvelous devoted friend.

My little angel, my guardian, my protector, my little sister.

"Go to the bridge," she said.

Wanting me to be happy.

Which was what she always wanted.

12. Roosevelt Hospital

Sunday, June 21st

At the hospital emergency desk, not far from Columbus Circle, Lolita told me the room number.

"313."

This was the same place where the guys had brought me ten days ago when the blood was gushing from a hole in my leg. It was also the same place where they'd brought John Lennon on the night he died.

Up on the third floor, I hustled down the corridor and found Eric Powers, dressed in his beat uniform, standing outside the door.

I didn't waste time.

"How'd he get to her?"

"She opened the dammed door!"

Eric was as irritated as I was.

"Is it bad?" I wondered, trying to prepare myself.

"Yeah, it's bad. *Real* bad."

He hesitated a moment, wondering if he should say what he wanted to say. Then he said it.

"Why the hell do you do it, Rick?"

I shrugged.

It was the job that nobody wanted.

Where the vics are often bloody and beaten.

Where the vics refuse to press charges.

Where there's often weapons at the scene.

Along with drugs and booze.

Where the cops are often attacked at the scene.

Where kids are often present.

Regarding all of which, the prosecutors seldom file charges.

(Less than 30% of the time.)

Regarding all of which, the prosecutors, even when they do file, usually let the perps plead out.

(Over 95% of the time.)

What else could I do but shrug?

I stepped inside room 313, and I saw what I could see of her, stretched out on the bed like a corpse in the morgue. Her face was mostly bandages, but I could still see her eyes, the left one was blood-red with subconjunctival hemorrhage, and I could also see some of the bruises over her cheekbones. There were various other purple and red contusions up and down her arms, and there was a brand new cast on her left wrist.

The bastard had broken her wrist!

Yeah, I felt sorry for her, but I was also mad as hell.

When she wasn't being beaten to a pulp by the likes of Lucas Baaden, Michelle Ramirez was a very attractive young Nuyorican in her mid-twenties, who taught third grade at OLQA in East Harlem, who'd met Baaden dancing one night with her girlfriends at Club Cache, who'd quickly fallen for his lies and his garbage.

She saw me coming into the room, but she said nothing.

I couldn't restrain myself.

"Did you really let him inside?"

All I could see were her eyes, and they were ashamed of themselves.

"Yes, he said he wanted to apologize."

"You fell for that!"

I was sorry that I said it even before I'd finished saying it. I was taking out my frustrations on the victim, even if she was, in this case, a world-class dumbass victim.

She said nothing.

"You should have called the precinct right away."

"I know."

"I didn't even know the bastard made bail."

"I know you didn't, Rick."

She wasn't blaming anyone but herself.

Then she started to cry, making a quick and ugly mess of her damaged eyes and her bright-white bandages. I handed her some tissues, so she could dab at herself, and I took her right hand into mine.

Trying to comfort her.

This one broke my heart. Yeah, sure, "keep your distance" from the vics, especially the pretty domestic-abuse vics, but it's easier said than done.

Yeah, this one broke my heart, but it was more than that, and I knew it. Right from the beginning, I'd felt myself oddly attracted to all of her loveliness and all of her lovely helplessness, and I sensed that it might have been reciprocated if I hadn't always pushed it from my mind, away from the both of us, thinking, before Alice came along, of Heather.

Thinking of Barnegat Light.

"I'll find him, Michelle. I promise."

Which didn't reassure her as much as I'd hoped.

It's true that I was known at Midtown and throughout the borough as the guy who always nailed the "beaters."

Diffusing the scene.

Getting witnesses to talk.

Getting dispositive photos. Injuries, etc.

Getting EPOs (restraining orders).

Getting, whenever possible, proof of the tangentials: intoxication, vandalism (smashing stuff), and child endangerment.

But Lucas Baaden had slipped through my hands.

Through the courts.

"I know you'll catch him, Rick. Eventually. But what if he finds me first? And what am I supposed to do when I get out of this place? I've got two little kids, and I can't just pick up and leave the city. Besides, he'd find me anyway."

"I know, Michelle, I'll think of something. Trust me."

"I know you will, Rick. I trust you, and I'm sorry to be such a baby, especially since everything's my fault."

"Everything's his fault. You didn't beat yourself, Michelle."

She nodded.

"Don't worry, I'll take care of you."

She lifted up my hand to her lips, and she kissed me gently. Then she looked into my eyes, and I remembered just how beautiful she was.

"Trust me, Michelle. He's got two priors, and he's shot a cop, and now he's done this. When I bust him, he's going upstream for a long, long time.

"How long?"
"Twenty years."
"That's a start."

13. The Vista

Sunday, June 21st

I was sitting on top of Vista Rock, the highest point in the park, not far from the castle. It was the place where I've always felt the most comfortable, all alone with myself and my own little thoughts, sitting high above the Ramble, high above the entire park, with a clear and distant view of the lovely Fifth Avenue skyline.

At the moment, as I did so often, I was watching the soaring birds. Maybe I couldn't recognize every single one of the two hundred species that either inhabited or regularly visited the park, but I knew an awful lot of them, and I was focused, this early afternoon, on a red-tailed hawk which was gliding majestically on the gentle breeze, beautifully and seemingly so carefree. For me, I suppose, the red-tails were always a symbol of the kind of freedom that

I could never know.

Soaring above us all, in graceful flight, with a kind of slow and deliberate serenity.

Of course, like so much else in this peculiar life of mine, it was all a mirage. Because there's nothing at all peaceful or serene about the soaring red-tails, who were birds of prey, raptors, deadly predators, the preferred hunters of most falconers, who could dive at over 120 miles-per-hour, pluck off some mindless chipmunk, squirrel, or other victim with their ready talons, and fly it away to be killed and then devoured.

Still warm.

So I tried to think about something else.

Something, anything, that wasn't you.

I thought about Christopher.

I thought about the afternoon we first met. When he'd asked my father if he could speak to his oldest daughter. I remembered how handsome he looked in his dark-blue Brooks Brothers suit; how gracious, even solicitous, he was; how he brought me a flower, a white lily; how he complimented my beautiful white dress; how I thought to myself that I must be the luckiest girl in the world; and how I felt, for the first time in my life, odd little stirrings in my heart, which felt so lovely, so magical.

I remembered all those first-ever young girl's

thoughts of the "might be's" of love. I remembered his politeness. I remembered the eager, innocent, and respectful look in his soulful eyes, and I remembered thinking to myself that this young extraordinary man would, if things continued on their natural course, treat me like a princess for the rest of my life, and it felt perfectly marvelous . . .

But you kept intruding.

You wouldn't leave me alone.

Some tough-guy "rough-around-the-edges" cop, who spent most of his time chasing violent criminals and getting himself shot in the leg, who'd somehow, irrevocably, instantly, altered my little universe and made my once-upon-a-time feelings for Christopher, though still undeniably real and sincere, seem like a tiny ripple on the calm surface of a pool compared to the violent tsunami whirling in my now conflicted heart.

I tried, again, to think of anything but you.

Remembering when I was a young girl, and how I loved reading the "decadent" poets. Those so-called "yellow decade" rhymers from England. I know! Don't laugh! (Assuming you even know who they are!) Yes, it's true, I've never been, in any way possible, the slightest bit decadent, and the very thought of such a horrible life-capitulation sends a rip down my spine. I've never (then or now) had any sympathy whatsoever for their showy alcoholic stupors or their drug-accelerated depressions. Which they pretended to somehow enjoy. But I did, nevertheless, love their pathetic sincerity. And I loved their ever-so-faint sanguinity in the midst of all their decadent squalors.

I loved poor Ernest the best of them all! (Ernest Dowson. Look him up!) Especially his two most famous poems, "Non Sum Qualis Eram Bonae Sub Regno Cynarae" and "Vitae Summa Brevis Spem Nos Vetat Incohare Longam," the latter of which, coming from Horace, I would translate, without much confidence in my rusty Latin, as: "The brevity of our lives prevents us from entertaining any enduring hopefulness."

Something like that.

The poem, just like our lives, is short, and its rhythms and rhymes make it so easy to memorize, and it also contains one of the most famous phrases in all of English-language literature:

"the days of wine and roses"

So I sat on top of Vista Rock, refusing to think about you, listening to the little quatrains rattling in my head:

They are not long, the weeping and the
  laughter,
Love and desire and hate:
I think they have no portion in us after
We pass the gate.

They are not long, the days of wine and
  roses:
Out of a misty dream
Our path emerges for a while, then closes
Within a dream.

Why would I like such a thing?

Sure, it's very beautifully written, beautifully constructed, but it's insistent on the fact that nothing, absolutely nothing, ever lasts, not even our most powerful emotions, our most powerful longings and lovings. Not even that extraordinary moment when I first saw you bleeding across Central Park West, not even when we first looked into each other's eyes at Umpire Rock, and the subsequent instantaneous inexplicable incomprehensible stupendous explosion, the devastating gush-and-rush implosion of desire that shocked awake my moribund heart.

So I thought about poor tubercular Ernest, ever-drinking, ever-pining after the young Adelaide, the unrequited love of his short life, longing for what he'd lost, longing, almost pathetically for something, anything, that was pure and innocent and deep and lasting.

But I still didn't buy it.

Or, at least, I didn't really care.

So what if nothing lasts?

We live right here, here-and-now, and even in my own weirdo here-and-now, which was like no other here-and-now in the entire history of the world, I'd, once again, let you right back inside my thoughts.

I'd let you intrude.

I'd given in to my weaker self.

I'd succumbed.

With pleasure.

14. Balcony Bridge

Sunday, June 21ˢᵗ

I was standing on Balcony Bridge in the late and muted afternoon sun on one of its two little "balconies," not far from Hernshead, not far from the Ladies Pavilion, overlooking the western half of the Lake, which many people claim is the absolute most beautiful and most scenic view of the Central Park Lake.

But I wasn't paying attention.

None.

"We need to get every cop, every park ranger, every cabbie, and every snitch looking for that bastard."

I was talking to Helen down at the precinct.

"He'll kill her the next time, Helen."

She didn't disagree.

"I think you're right, Ricky."

"I'm sure I can count on you to fire up the boys, Helen, but don't tell the chief that I've been sticking my nose in. As a matter of fact, don't even tell him that I'm in the loop."

"Don't worry, Rick."

She always seemed to understand everything.

"Sometimes this job really sucks," I said.

I guess I was feeling sorry for myself.

"Yes, but sometimes it works."

When I didn't agree, she changed the subject.

"What's with you and the girl?"

"What girl, Miss Busybody?"

We laughed, and I hung up the phone.

Finally, I could take a moment's moment to look at the Lake, at its serene blue waters, at the surrounding lush greens of the trees, and try to enjoy the natural beauty of the places around me.

Then something even more marvelous caught my eye.

She was standing, suddenly, right next to me.

As if from nowhere.

Immediately, all the beauties of the park, of nature itself, of everything lovely in this wide and fallen world were instantly moot, insignificant, and forgotten.

She wore a light-and-white summer dress with light-green trim, with light-green Mary Janes, with a light-green ribbon in her thick, dark, ever-cascading hair.

"Maybe you *are* a ghost," I said.

"Maybe I am."

She smiled.

"I didn't know if you'd come," I said rather stupidly.

"Neither did I."

I tried to be serious.

"Don't run away from me again."

When she didn't respond, I got a hell of a lot more serious. I stepped forward and kissed her on the mouth, gently, which I won't bother to attempt to explain or describe, except to say that nothing in my previous pointless existence had ever been so lovely or so heart-crushingly significant.

She didn't resist.

When I forced myself to stop, she looked away, as if confused, saying, almost to herself.

"I really don't do that kind of thing."

Which seemed rather peculiar.

"Why not, Alice? Was it bad?"

"No, it was wonderful, but isn't that exactly the problem?"

Which confused me even more.

"What problem?"

She just shook her head, as if to say that I could

never understand.

Maybe I couldn't.

"Alice?"

She turned back to look directly into my eyes, and I told her what I didn't know that she'd already heard at the zoo on Nikki's speakerphone.

"I've fallen in love with you."

She said nothing.

"It's really that simple," I insisted, gently, simply.

"But it's not simple, Rick. As a matter of fact, it's perfectly ridiculous. You don't even know me!"

"Then tell me about yourself. I want to know everything. Everything."

Worn-out, she gave in.

Or seemed to.

"All right, Rick. But not today."

All right, I thought to myself, I can be patient. Most New Jersey guys know nothing about patience, but being a cop in the city has forced me to learn about the most impossible of all the virtues.

She smiled, rather mischievously, and I liked it.

"Give me your wallet," she said.

I did as I was told, and she sat down on the balcony bench, facing the waters, and started, quite happily, snooping through my wallet.

"It might come as a shock to the likes of you," I

pointed out, "but all of my IDs are real."

When she smiled again, I sat down beside her.

Eventually, she came across the photograph of a perfectly lovely, smiling, young woman in a white tennis sweater.

Then she looked at me inquisitively, and I told her.

"She was my girlfriend, Alice. Actually, she was closer to being my fiancée. Her name was Heather MacMaster. We met a few years ago when I was taking criminal justice courses at NYU, when she was studying art history."

"What happened?"

"She drowned two years ago in a jet-skiing accident off Barnegat Light."

"I'm so sorry, Rick. She's so lovely. So beautiful!"

I thought she might cry, but she caught herself, and I tried to be as honest as I could.

"I'm not ashamed to admit that it's been a tough two years."

She understood.

She put the photo back in its place carefully, then handed me my wallet.

"Have you been able to deal with it, Rick?"

She asked it like someone who's also had a lot to deal with.

Like someone who found it easy to commiserate.

"Yeah, especially recently, especially since I got shot in the leg. That woke me up a bit."

I looked directly at Alice.

"Especially since I met you."

Once again, Alice seemed a bit overwhelmed by everything, and I was afraid that she might start crying, but she didn't.

Finally, she stood up in front of me.

"Why don't we take a walk somewhere? Maybe over to the Fountain?"

"Anywhere you want," I said. "Anywhere."

I meant it, and she knew I meant it.

We headed southeast, strolling slowly, casually, along the west side of the Lake, and she took my arm so gently that I barely noticed it. Just like any other proper young lady who was being escorted through the park.

But she was curious about something.

"Where's Barnegat Light?"

I was surprised.

"At the Jersey Shore. Haven't you been there?"

"No, I haven't. I haven't been very many places at all."

"Good! I'll take you there myself. I'll also take you to Rio, and the Bahamas, and Venice, and Waikiki! What do you think of that?"

She smiled.

She liked the idea.

We both did.

We passed Wagner Cove, walked the path along Terrace Drive, and headed toward Bethesda Terrace, where we went down the steps to the fountain.

To the most famous fountain in the Park.

In all of New York City.

In all of America.

(Yeah, sure, the Bellagio in Vegas might disagree, but they'd be wrong.)

To what was known as the "Heart of the Park."

Where we mixed in with lots of New Yorkers relaxing in the late afternoon, and with lots of tourists endlessly taking photos of the statue of the Angel of the Waters, high above the upper basin, as the fountain's waters gently flowed over its edges to the pool below.

The waters, as they always did, murmured a bit, quite serenely. Alice stopped and did some more wondering.

"Tell me more about Richard Kincaid."

"I've already told you the whole story: my parents, the crash, the foster homes, baseball, Rutgers, the Academy. That's it. That's all there is."

"Why domestic abuse?"

I told her.

"Because I'd seen some of it when I was a kid at one of the foster homes. It was over in Brooklyn, and the foster guy came home drunk one night, and he started yelling at our foster mom, whom we all liked quite a bit. I was about eight at the time, the oldest of the kids, and I definitely didn't like what was happening. In no time, the pig started pounding on our foster mom, whose name was Victoria, so I tried to pull him off, but he knocked me hard, right against the wall, where I smashed the back of my head. I was bleeding, but I was still conscious, so I crawled over to her purse, pulled out her cell, and dialed 911."

"What happened?"

"Not much. She wouldn't press charges, and me and the rest of the kids were immediately moved to different foster homes."

"I'm sorry, Rick."

I shrugged.

"It was just something that happened to me when I was a kid. I never felt especially traumatized about it, but I've never forgotten it, and I guess, eventually, I decided that I should try and help the defenseless women who refuse to help themselves."

"Did you ever see Victoria again?"

"No, but I looked her up about two years ago, not long after Heather died, but she'd also died."

"From abuse?"

"From cancer."

She seemed greatly affected.

"This is getting quite unromantic," I pointed out, pointing out the obvious.

"I know, but I'm the one who asked."

We walked back to the top of the terrace stairs, moving rather thoughtlessly east, toward Fifth Avenue.

Then thunder cracked.

Maybe "boomed" would be a better way to put it.

In unison, we both looked up at the sky, as people always do, even though there wasn't very much to see, just an ever-graying overcast.

Nothing that seemed to indicate an immediate thunderstorm.

Then it started pouring.

We were standing near the Hunt Memorial on Fifth, just north of 70th, which offered nothing in the way of shelter, so I tried holding my windbreaker over our heads, but it was pouring, and the wind was gusting, and all my efforts were useless, and we both got soaked.

Instantly.

Even Alice's thick dark hair was saturated and furiously dripping, and the rain was so unrelenting that we could barely open our eyes.

Which was both confusing and disorienting.

Which seemed to strike her as quite humorous, and she laughed her lovely laugh, with her pretty eyes shut to the rain.

I got an idea.

"Come on, let's get out of this mess! Let's go over to the Frick."

I put my arm around her shoulder and started gently guiding her toward the curb, toward Fifth Avenue.

"I can't," she said softly, oddly.

Which I didn't take seriously.

"Come on," I encouraged her, "it's right across the street, and you're completely soaked!"

We took a step forward, as she instantly collapsed in my arms. Since I was already holding her, I managed to keep her from crashing to the pavement beneath us, but she was essentially dead weight, and I had to lower her carefully to the ground, which, of course, was covered with an ever-swirling sheet of the rapidly falling rain.

I was astonished.

Terrified.

Kneeling over her, I put my arm under her neck and her shoulders to prop her head up, above the puddling pavement.

I rocked her gently.

"Alice!"

But her eyes were still closed, and the rains were still whirling around us.

When she didn't respond, I checked the pulse at her neck, and I could feel the steady beating of her heart.

"Alice! What's going on?"

No response.

I pulled out my cell to call for the EMTs.

But I hesitated for some inexplicable reason, looking down at her lovely wet face, and rather impulsively, I kissed her on her rain-soaked lips.

Instantly, she opened her eyes.

Like Snow White.

Like Sleeping Beauty.

A bit groggy.

"Are you all right?" I asked, rather stupidly.

"I can't leave the park."

She said it gently, as if it explained everything. As if it revealed a long-concealed confidence that clarified everything.

I was, of course, completely baffled.

But something must have made some kind of sense deep within the more secretive and subtle parts of my brain.

"You live in the park?"

"Yes."

All right.

Fine.

It was just that simple.

"For how long?"

"Ten years."

I didn't bother to speculate about whether it might be possible, and I didn't make any further attempts to fathom whatever it might have meant, I was just happy (that's the only word that seems to fit) that she was awake again and seemingly all right and slowly becoming herself again.

She looked into my eyes, and I realized that the thunderstorm was gradually dissipating.

<u>15. The Barrier</u>

Sunday, June 21st

We tried!

Of course, we tried!

Many many times, my love.

Over and over and over.

So many times, especially in the beginning, and then, later, every single year on Nikki's birthday.

For the past nine years.

"It'll work this time," she'd always say, never really believing it. So we'd go over to one of the four edges of the park, maybe CP West, or 59th, or Fifth, or sometimes 110th.

"You ready?"

Then Nikki would hold me tight. With her right arm around my waist, back when she was still just a little girl, and we'd wait for a break in the traffic. Then we'd step towards the curb together, and I'd collapse, and she'd catch me every single time and hold me, then gently lay me down on the sidewalk.

Unconscious.

"Everything's all right," she'd tell all the nice people who'd stop and offer to help. "She's fine. She just needs some rest." Eventually, the nice people would move along, back into their lives, mixing in with all the ones who'd looked away and didn't want to get involved.

"So what's it like?" she'd ask, in those early days.

Which, I'm quite sure, you've been wondering yourself.

The truth is, love, it's not really as bad as it looks, as long as I don't crash down on the pavement! I just go blank. Totally dark. It doesn't hurt at all. There's absolutely no pain. None. And there's no disconcerting dreams or creepy nightmares racing through my shut-off mind. Just a black and silent blankness. Which isn't unpleasant. Not in the least. Then, as Nikki would pull me back from the curb, which must have been quite a sight when she was twelve years old, my eyes would suddenly pop open as if nothing at all had happened.

"You look funny."

She was right.

Because I always came back a little groggy, a

little bit confused. But eventually I'd realize where I was, lying on my back on some New York City sidewalk, and I'd feel fine.

With no repercussions.

Nothing.

Naturally, as time went by, we got more inventive.

One year, Nikki got the brilliant idea to have me sit on a sheet of cardboard so I could be slowly pulled to the curb. As if, I suppose, we were somehow outwitting "whatever" was doing whatever it was that was being done to me.

"What'll people think?" I wondered.

"Who cares?" Nikki assured me. "It's New York. Weird stuff happens all the time."

Then she'd think a little bit harder.

"Maybe they'll think it's performance art."

I laughed. Just as I always laughed at her lovely earnestness and her little girl's determination.

So she bought some rope from the hardware store, using the lunch money that she'd been saving in her little Mickey Mouse piggy bank, and she hired a few big guys from the park, and she tied the rope around my waist, and I sat down on a big sheet of cardboard, and she gave the boys the signal, and they started pulling me, very slowly, towards the street, until, suddenly, I went dark.

As always, Nikki was right there to catch me before I slumped over and hit the pavement.

The following year, she paid some other big guys to carry me across the threshold, which we always called "the barrier," which seemed to be about two feet from the edge of the curb. To be honest, I really didn't like the idea of some guys I didn't even know touching me and holding me.

In truth, even if I did know them, I wouldn't have liked them touching me or holding me.

"Oh, don't be such a prude," she'd say with her little girl's worldliness.

So I over-dressed, wrapped myself in a blanket, and the guys picked me up and started carrying me towards 110th, until all three of us went blank. Nikki, of course, caught me, but the other two guys crashed to the pavement, and one of them scraped his forehead pretty bad.

But they were good sports about it, although whatever had happened to them clearly spooked them a bit, so they took their cash and ducked back into the park.

Then we tried a bike, which was as foolish as it sounds, and much too dangerous.

"No more of that," we both decided.

Then we tried a Central Park horse-and-carriage, but when I conked out in the carriage, the horse stopped in its tracks, right where it was, and to the complete bafflement of its driver, absolutely refused to move forward.

So the old guy offered Nikki her money back, and he was glad to get rid of us.

Then there were the multiple taxi attempts.

Nikki and I would get in the back of a cab on Terrace Drive, and she'd say "Lincoln Center," as casually as possible, once again trying to outwit whatever it was that was keeping me in the park, and the cabbie would start heading towards West 72nd Street, but a few feet short of CP West, his engine would fail, and he'd get out of the cab, amid all the furious honking horns and the unpleasant yellings and cursings, and lift up the taxi's hood and find nothing wrong.

"Put it in reverse," Nikki would tell him, which I never actually heard since I was, at the moment, unconscious, and the cabbie, in frustration, would finally decide to do whatever the bossy little girl told him to do, who was still sitting in his back seat propping up her "sleeping" friend, and the engine would miraculously start, and the cab would back up, and I'd wake up again. Then we'd get out of the cab and watch the cabbie drive away, more than glad to put us in his rear-view mirror.

In silence, Nikki and I would find a nearby bench

and sit down next to each other.

But she was irrepressible.

"It'll work next year," she'd say with a child's confidence. With a child's conviction.

Then she'd take my hand and look into my eyes.

"You're quite the weirdo, Alice."

And we'd laugh.

Happily.

What else could we do?

And, yes, yes, yes, my love, it was all terribly terribly frustrating.

It's true that I absolutely love the park, but I can't tell you how much I would have loved to go outside its boundaries sometimes, beyond the "barrier," and see the rest of this amazing city that completely surrounded me, and see the rest of the outlying world that also surrounded me, and be like the red-tail hawk, having the freedom to effortlessly glide whenever I wished, away and beyond and over the extremities of my beautiful park.

But we don't always get what we want.

Do we, love?

<u>16. Kiss</u>

Sunday, June 21st

Alice was still lying right beneath me on the soaking wet pavement.

She was looking into my eyes with what could only be described as love.

"You know what?"

I had no idea.

(I really didn't.)

"What?"

"I've only been kissed once in my life."

It seemed preposterous.

"By you."

I smiled.

Then I almost laughed.

"Do you really expect me to believe that?"

She was serious.

Very serious.

"I expect you to believe everything I tell you."

Which seemed fair, no matter how ridiculous, if you really love someone.

"OK, I will," I assured her.

"Good."

I smiled again.

"Did you like it?" I asked.

Meaning the kiss, which she fully understood, smiling as well.

"Very much. Let's try it again."

I didn't tell her, until later, that I'd already kissed her a few moments earlier.

Then, for the third time, I kissed her lovely mouth, in a kind of paradisal whirl of sensations, beneath the fastly-fading thunderstorm.

"How was that?" I asked.

"Wonderful."

She smiled mischievously.

"But maybe, if it's not too much to ask, you could help me get up from this soaking-wet pavement."

She seemed to be herself again.

We got ourselves upright and immediately re-entered the now-deserted park at 69th Street. The whole time, I kept my arm around her, and she held to me tightly.

It felt marvelous.

"Are you sure you don't need a medic?" I wondered, still concerned.

"I *am* a medic, Rick, and I assure you I'm fine. It's happened before."

I didn't bother to ask what *it* was. At least, not for now.

"Where should we go?" I wondered, thinking of the Bandshell.

"The Bandshell," she said.

<u>17. The Kiss</u>

Sunday, June 21st

I supposed I should have been somewhat embarrassed.

After all, what would you think?

A girl who's never been kissed!

But that's how I was raised, and even the past ten years in the park had done nothing to change it, since every bit of that time I was hiding, ducking, sneaking, and avoiding.

Especially men.

Which, of course, reinforced (what shall I call it?) my innocence. Because every minute of every day, there was always the reasonable fear of exposure, of discovery, and I was compelled to hide-and-wait for as long as was necessary, to keep myself, as much as possible, the exact same way that I was back then. So that I'd be ready, eventually, to do whatever it was I had to do.

So any kind of lover, or boyfriend, or suitor, or paramour was absolutely out of the question, despite all of Nikki's proddings and all of her disastrous little attempts to serve as my personal matchmaker. I was, I knew, in some kind of inexplicable hiatus, quarantining myself from the world, and especially from the peculiar and often quite crude and rude and undignified men of this bizarre world that I'd somehow stumbled into.

Then seemingly from nowhere, there was you.

Why did you seem so different?

Why did I recognize it the very first moment I saw you?

Why did I let you hold me?

Why did I let you kiss me?

And when I did, why did it feel like what one of those silly love poets once described:

. . . how cosmic space retracts itself in scale,
and time, self-destructively, swallows its tail.

18. Naumburg Bandshell

Sunday, June 21st

She was asleep in my arms.

Gently.

We were sitting on the floor of the old bandshell, beneath the high overhang, within the Wisteria Pergola. We were facing the empty Central Park Mall, facing the statue of Beethoven. In the distant past, Irving Berlin had performed here, and John Philip Sousa, and Duke Ellington. Martin Luther King had once spoken here, and John Lennon was eulogized here after the shooting.

The summer skies had darkened considerably, and the rains were schizophrenically intermittent, from light misty drizzles to sudden violent downpours, with loudly cracking reverberating thunders and brilliant flashes of lightning.

After what she called her "little episode" over on

Fifth Avenue, Alice was more than a bit weary and worn-out, so we made our way to the bandshell, talked a bit, mostly about the park itself, and soon she was asleep in my arms. It was probably the most comfortable and content I'd ever felt in my entire life. Holding her close to me, against me, as time slowly passed, passing by timelessly.

The minutes, the hours, and, now, the falling twilight.

Was it possible that she really lived in the park? For ten years? It seemed preposterous. I was aware, of course, that, on occasion, a few of the park's employees were allowed to live in the park for the duration of certain short-term projects, but it was never more than a few people, and I'd already seen the current list of four at the CP Administration Office.

Alice definitely wasn't on the list.

I looked out at the park.

I love the park in the rain, and I especially love it in the twilight. Actually, I love it all the time, and I knew it well. *Very* well. I might not have been "some kind of expert" like the lovely girl lying in my arms, but I'd spent a great deal of time wandering its 843 acres during the past two years.

Ever since Heather's accident.

Ever since her death.

Every day, I'd do my bit at the precinct or out on the Midtown streets, and then later, afterwards, maybe just to avoid going home to my empty apartment at Alwyn Court, I'd wander around the park.

Under the elms, past the monuments, up through the Ramble, around the reservoir. Etc.

Everywhere.

I hadn't had to deal with death since I was seven years old when my grandmother died, and I didn't have a clue how to react. Sometimes I'd drive over to the beaches at Barnegat Light, but mostly, more helpfully, I'd wander around the park trying to appreciate it, trying to appreciate life itself, trying to be grateful for my lonely life, despite the pains in my heart, despite the hollowness of my life, trying not to feel sorry for myself.

Oddly enough, Heather and I had never spent much time in the park together. Back during our NYU days, she was living down in the Village, and we'd sometimes hang out in Washington Square, or, more often, we'd go down to Battery Park and stare at the lady in the harbor. Later, when she moved back to Hoboken, we'd mostly meet in Midtown, and we'd often go sit together in Bryant Park.

So those were the "Heather" parks: the Bryant, the Battery, and Washington Square.

But this park, the most amazingly fantastic inner-city park in the world, was, of course, the "Alice" park.

After only three days.

She stirred a bit in my arms, snuggling close, and I wished that it could last forever.

But of course, nothing lasts forever.

She stirred again, opened her eyes, and looked into mine. I wondered if she'd be uncomfortable with our closeness, our intimacy, but she seemed perfectly content.

"Have you been holding me?" she wondered, groggily, stupidly.

"Yes."

When I smiled, she smiled as well.

"Are you warm enough?" I wondered.

"I'm fine."

"You've slept through some really loud thunderclaps."

"Well, I haven't been getting much sleep recently, and I guess you're a pretty comfortable pillow."

"Anytime."

She sat up and looked at her park.

"I love the twilight."

"Me too."

"How long have we been sitting here?"

"It was timeless."

She smiled again.

"All right, wiseguy."

She looked down at her little white watch, but I beat her to it.

"Over three hours."

When she nodded, I got romantic.

Or, at least, I tried.

Doing the best that someone like me was capable of.

"I could hold you forever."

She liked it, and I loved that she liked it, but I could tell that she would, once again, very soon, be trying to leave me.

"Do you remember what happened?"

She didn't respond. She seemed momentarily distracted, so I tried again.

Gently.

"You need to tell me what happened, Alice. You need to tell me the truth. You need to tell me everything."

Instantly, I could tell that we were suddenly back in mystery mode.

Once again, she'd become the lovely princess of subterfuge. Not to mention evasiveness.

"I can't. Not today, Rick. Please, I told you that earlier."

Then, as if attempting to smooth it all over, she kissed my forehead, which felt lovely.

"Thanks for taking care of me, Rick, but I have to go home."

She stood up and straightened out her still-damp summer dress.

"I thought you lived in the park?"

She looked at me like I was crazy.

Like I was an idiot.

She even smiled at my foolishness, almost patronizingly.

"What!?"

I stood up, in my usual state of confusion, with a bit of irritation as well.

"Well, that's what you told me earlier."

"That's perfectly ridiculous, Rick! Nobody lives in the park. Besides, why would you believe anything a woman says after she's had a fainting spell."

"A 'fainting spell'?"

Who talks like that?

What planet did this girl come from?

Alice ignored me and kept going.

"I have no idea what I told you when I was barely conscious, Rick, but I live over on Lexington, and I need to catch a cab right away and get myself home."

Her little pal Nikki lived over on Lexington, but

I still didn't believe her, although I did believe that pressing the issue right now would get me nowhere. So I decided, once again, to be patient.

We walked to Terrace Drive in silence, holding hands, and she hailed the first cab that came along.

I stayed close, not only to be close to her, but to watch carefully whatever would happen next.

The taxi pulled over, I opened the back-seat door, and Alice hugged me quickly and got inside.

She looked into my eyes.

"Thanks so much, Rick, for everything. It was wonderful."

Which was fine with me, but I still didn't shut the door. Finally, she did what I wanted her to do. She gave the cabbie her destination.

"316 Lexington."

Nikki lived in the Barrio, not down in the 300's. Once again, I didn't believe her, but at the moment, I didn't care that much because I was kissing her lovely lips, and all the obfuscations, misdirections, and prevarications were momentarily meaningless.

Of no consequence.

"Don't go," I tried.

To no avail, of course.

"I have to go, Rick."

"Why?"

"Not now, Rick. Please."

When I saw the sadness in her eyes, which was the last thing I ever wanted to see, I backed off.

"Meet me tomorrow," I insisted.

"I will, Rick. I'll call you tomorrow morning."

Which was somewhat reassuring, somewhat satisfying.

The cabbie had had enough.

"Is the door stuck?"

Actually, I think there was an expletive in there between the word "the" and the word "door," and even though I appreciated his wiseassedness, I ignored him.

Completely.

"Is that a promise?"

She looked into my eyes again, as if she knew that it made me weak and pliable and, yes, even helpless.

"It's a promise."

She said it with such a depth of sincerity that it seemed to be the most sincere promise ever uttered by a human being on the surface of planet earth.

I nodded, shut the door, and the cab took off, heading toward CP West. Suddenly, I felt terribly alone. It was, of course, a much different "alone" than I'd felt that day when the chief had called me into his office, on that ugly Saturday two years ago, and told me about Barnegat Light. Much different than the subsequent "alone" that I'd been feeling ever since.

Until Umpire Rock.

But it was still a rather depressing "alone" nevertheless.

Mindlessly, I walked over to the terrace and looked down at the fountain. The skies were at it again, but I stood there impervious to the lightly falling rain and marveled at the beauty of the "heart of the park," even with everyone gone, even without all the loving lovers who loved the fountain, even without Alice Appleton.

Who was gone away.

Once again.

Somewhere.

But I decided not to feel sorry for myself, as I turned around and walked down the mostly deserted mall. As the rains, once again, began letting up, I sat down on "my bench" near the Sixth Avenue entrance at Central Park South, being Bench #00731, which was a block away from my apartment at Alwyn Court.

This was where I always ended up after my rambles through the park. Where I could mull over my cases, where I could rethink my past, where I could remember Heather and our good times together, where I could sometimes think about nothing at all, just sitting here, all alone, on Bench

#00731, wrapped within my own little universe.

Where, now, I could think of her.

Of Alice.

Of the good, the bad, and the inexplicable.

There were, I'd once read somewhere, 9,485 benches in Central Park, and almost half of them had little metal plaques attached. With little tributes, little memorials, little remembrances, little quotes. Some of the quotes are well-known, while others are completely unknown. I'd chosen this particular bench to be my personal bench, not just because it was so convenient and close to home, but because of its little inscription, which I often thought about while I was sitting here, which I always found intriguing, which I never fully understood:

> *This is a place to dream things*
> *that never were – and ask why not.*

<u>19. The Taxi</u>

Sunday, June 21st

I sat in the back of the cab and cried, it was a terrible cry, it was an angry-at-the-universe cry.

I was grateful that the cabbie had no interest whatsoever, that he paid no attention at all.

20. Alwyn Court

Monday, June 22nd

The city sun was shining through my window, high atop Alwyn Court, not far from Carnegie Hall.

When I opened my eyes, I didn't see Willie Mays. Instead, there was a lovely Latina sitting on the edge of my bed, wearing a soft cotton nightgown, gently shaking my uninjured leg.

"Wake up, Rick."

As my vision cleared, I could see her bruises.

I could also see that she was holding the cordless kitchen phone.

"There's a call for you."

Which had woken me up.

I took the phone from Michelle and sat up in bed beside her.

She smelled lovely, like coconut.

I was wearing my usual "bedtimes": navy sweat-shorts and a navy NYPD t-shirt.

"Yeah?"

"Rick?"

It was Alice. I was excited, but concerned. There was something "off" in her voice, and it wasn't just that she'd called me early in the morning and another woman had answered the phone.

I tried to be upbeat.

"Who's the early bird?"

"It's Alice."

As if I didn't know.

"I thought it was somebody else. Maybe the prettiest girl in the world."

Which didn't seem to bother Michelle at all, but it seemed to knock back Alice, who didn't respond.

"All right, Alice, tell me what's wrong."

She told me.

"I'm sorry, Rick, but I can't see you anymore."

It sounded rather apocalyptic.

She tried to explain.

Inadequately.

"It's not your fault, Rick. It's all mine, and I'm sorry, and I hope you'll forgive me."

I knew exactly what she was planning to do next.

"Don't hang up that phone!"

The line went dead.

Immediately, I called her back, but it rang and

rang and rang. Fed up, moronically, I threw the phone across the room where it smashed into the closet door, making a particularly loud crack before it fell to the floor in several pieces.

Michelle put a comforting hand on my thigh.

"I'm sorry, Rick."

I didn't know what to say, so I said, "Damn it!"

As if that helped.

Then I looked over at the shattered phone lying in pieces on the bedroom floor, and I realized what I might have done.

"I hope I didn't wake up the kids."

"Don't worry, Rick, they can sleep through anything."

So we sat there together, alone, trapped within our own unsettling thoughts.

<u>21. The Crying</u>

Monday, June 22nd

I hung up the phone, Nikki's cell, and I cried again, even though I'd determined not to, even though I'm a very determined person, even though Nikki says I'm the most determined person on planet earth, assuming that I really am, in fact, on planet earth.

22. Cop Cot

Monday, June 22nd

I was lost in thoughts.

I was sitting, not that far from my favorite bench, within the park's weird, little, open-aired, rustic wooden cottage, which, from a distance, looked like it was made of sticks, like the one the dumb little pig built before the Big Bad Wolf blew it down.

I was holding her photograph.

Earlier I'd gone over to 316 Lexington, which, as it turns out, is a little restaurant called Café del Amore, and, of course, nobody in the restaurant and nobody who lived in any of the apartments upstairs had ever heard of "Alice Appleton" or seen the girl in the surveillance photo.

I believed them.

I also believed the cabbie.

Last night, I'd memorized his plate as he was

driving Alice away from me on Terrace Drive, and I tracked him down this morning.

"Hell, we didn't even get to CP West! She changed her mind, told me to pull over, apologized too much, then gave me a twenty."

"Anything else?"

"Yah, she's a very pretty girl, but I'm sure you know that already. *Very* pretty. But the whole thing seemed a little bit 'off' to me, if you know what I mean."

I knew what he meant.

I gave him two more twenties, and I went over to my "thinking" bench to mull it over. Then I came over here to the house of twigs.

To think about it some more.

Helen arrived. She was carrying, as always, her thin, little, black-leather attaché case, and she put an immediate end to all my musings.

"Is someone brooding?" she asked, as if life was way too short to condone such an indulgence, such an impertinence.

"I guess he was," I admitted, "but it's over."

"Good."

She sat down next to me on one of the wooden benches, unzipped her attaché case, and pulled out a file.

"What's happening with Baaden?" I asked.

"He was spotted at a club in Jersey City last night."

"That's it?"

I didn't hide my frustration.

"Yes, but don't worry, Rick. He'll be back. He won't be able to resist the soccer tournament on Thursday."

"Is he really that stupid?"

Helen looked at me like *I* was the stupid one, which I guess I was, and she didn't even bother to respond. Instead, she looked at me with her sly little "I know what's going on" smile.

"By the way, Eric Powers stopped off at Michelle's apartment this morning, and she and the kids are gone. But I'm sure you don't know anything about that."

"Yeah," I said, "I'm sure I don't."

Helen paused for a moment, looking out over the Pond, which lay beneath us.

"It's very lovely here, Rick."

Then she looked around, at the little house of twigs.

The Cop Cot.

"What's it mean anyway? I'm sure you know."

"It's Scottish, maybe Gaelic. It means 'the little house on the crest of the hill,' even though it's sitting on solid rock."

"Why do we always meet here, Rick?"

Which was one of my last few remaining ties to a distant past.

"On the day my parents were married at St. Pat's, they came over here for some extra wedding pictures."

"What a wonderful idea!"

"I still have a few."

"Is that one of them?"

Meaning the one I was holding in my hand.

"No, it's the shot of Alice from the surveillance video."

I handed the photo to Helen, and she looked it over carefully.

Amazed.

"That's the girl I saw on Central Park West! On the night you were shot!"

"What?"

"It's her, Rick!"

"Are you sure?"

"Yes. As soon as I heard you were hit, I rushed up to 68th, but the boys had already brought you down from the rooftop, and they were shoving you into an ambulance."

"Yeah," I remembered, "then someone came over and kissed me on the forehead."

"Of course, I did. I was terrified, Rick. We all

were, but I was greatly relieved to see that it was just a leg shot."

"Yeah, nothing to worry about."

She ignored me.

"Then, while they were packing you into the ambulance, I glanced across CP West for some inexplicable reason, and I saw her standing there. Why I looked, and why she stood out from all the other people watching from across the street, I have no idea. She was watching intently, wearing a parkie uniform of some kind, and she clearly wanted to cross the street. Finally, she stepped forward and collapsed. Instantly. I was shocked. Fortunately, she seemed to fall straight down to the pavement, as if on top of herself, if that makes any sense, and she didn't hit her head on the ground. Naturally, I was very concerned, and since your ambulance had already taken off, I waited for a gap in the traffic, which, of course, took forever, then I crossed the street. By the time I got there, several bystanders had already helped her to her feet, and she immediately, but rather unsteadily, walked into the park and disappeared. It was very odd, Rickie, and very concerning, but I didn't go after her. Instead, I hailed a cab and followed you to the emergency room."

I was amazed.

"She never left the park."

Which I said to myself, which must have seemed odd to Helen, who must have assumed it was a question.

"No, Rick, she didn't."

"Maybe she knew who I was," I speculated. "Maybe it was no coincidence that we met at Umpire Rock."

She caught on immediately.

"Maybe she was watching the baseball game?"

"Softball game."

"Maybe she's been following you, Rick."

"Maybe."

Then she changed the subject a bit.

"She's very beautiful."

"Yeah, I've noticed."

We sat there for a moment, thinking it over, uselessly speculating in silence. Finally, it was time to get down to business.

"So what have you got?"

She opened her folder, and she handed me some old clippings and photographs.

"Lots of stuff, Rick. At least, on the Appletons. They were a very successful family of book publishers, who published all kinds of famous stuff: Kipling, *The Red Badge of Courage*, Lewis Carroll, *Uncle Remus*, Arthur Conan Doyle, Henry James, and tons of other stuff.

"Lewis Carroll?"

"Yeah. Why?"

I just shrugged.

"What else?"

"Most of the family drowned in 1915 in the Hudson River after the wedding of their youngest daughter, Hester Appleton. It was terrible, Rick. That's the clipping from *The New York Times*."

Quickly, I scanned through the clipping and started browsing through the old photos.

Then I saw it.

Since it's impossible to describe how I felt at the time, I won't bother.

Let's leave it at "stunned."

"What is it, Rick?"

"It's her."

Which seemed preposterous.

Which *was* preposterous.

Alice, wearing a long-and-lovely old-fashioned frilly white dress, was standing and smiling between two younger girls, most probably her twin sisters. All of them were dressed-to-the-nines with white bonnets and white parasols. Right behind them was the Bethesda Fountain.

I handed the photo to Helen.

She was flabbergasted, maybe for the first time in her life.

"It's her, Rick! It's definitely her!"

She turned the photo over and read the handwritten date on the back.

"This picture was taken in 1905. What's going on, Rick? Things are getting really creepy."

I had a more important question.

"What happened to Alice?"

"It's right here in one of the obituaries."

She pulled an old yellow clipping from her file and scanned it quickly.

"Dear Lord! She drowned right here in Central Park, Rickie! Over at the Lake, near Hernshead. She was, according to this, trying to rescue her little cousin."

Helen read off the name.

"James Wellington."

At this point, I guess I was beyond being surprised.

"When?"

She found the date.

"June 25th, 1905."

I double-checked with the *Times* article.

"Her family died on June 25th, 1915."

"Exactly ten years later, Rick! That's hard to believe."

It was all "hard to believe."

I read a bit from the *Times* article.

Out loud.

"'After the boat capsized in the Hudson, all the members of the Appleton family were drowned in the rapid river current. At approximately 2:00 in the afternoon.'"

I looked over at Helen.

"What time did Alice drown?"

She scanned through Alice's obituary.

Stunned once again.

"2:00!"

23. The Waking

Sunday, June 25th

"Are you dead?"

I wasn't.

But I was still trapped inside some kind of peculiar yet-not-quite terrifying blackness.

Someone was brushing the wet hair away from my eyes.

Gently.

"You're very beautiful."

I opened my eyes, and I saw the pretty little immigrant girl, maybe twelve years old, kneeling above me. She had a child's happy smile on her child's happy face, as if she'd discovered some kind of exciting buried treasure, and she wore a much-too-tight black shirt with huge white letters printed across the front: "IF LOST RETURN TO THE CENTRAL PARK ZOO"

It was very strange, of course, and I was totally confused and disoriented. It seemed as though I was lying on the bank of the Lake in the middle of Central Park, and I was completely soaked, completely drenched, and both my hair and my lovely dress were a soggy mess.

I had no idea what was happening, or what had happened, so I sat up and looked out at the Lake.

Stunned.

Then I remembered.

"Where's Jimmy?"

I panicked, trying to stand up, but I was too discombobulated.

I looked up.

At the little girl.

"Is he all right?"

She shrugged.

Just like a little girl.

"Was he rescued?" I asked her nervously, hopefully, thinking that somehow I must have been rescued as well.

Maybe even by the little girl, although she seemed too little, too young.

"Who?"

"Jimmy?"

"Who's Jimmy?"

"The little boy."

"There's no little boy. Just you and me. I saw you floating in the Lake, in that crazy white dress, and I waded in and pulled you to shore. There was no little boy."

"Are you sure?"

"Yeah. There's no one here but you and me."

So maybe Jimmy had already made it safely to shore. Maybe he was all right.

I was relieved.

Somewhat.

Yet not completely.

What in the world was going on in my life?

What was happening?

Then, as if from nowhere, I heard the most peculiar music, with pounding percussion and a singer who seemed to be singing in some kind of foreign language, but not one that I recognized, and it seemed to be emanating from the little girl!

But her lips weren't moving.

When she saw my confusion, she pulled out a thin, damp, tiny box from her back pocket, and the music, impossibly, was coming from within the tiny box.

"What's that?"

"La India," she said.

Which made no sense.

She held up her little box, right in front of me,

and I could see a woman singing her mysterious song on the surface of the little box.

She was actually moving!

"What's that?"

Now it was her turn to be confused.

"My cell," she said.

As if it was obvious.

As if it resolved the issue.

I looked around me.

Above me.

At the eastern edge of the park, I could see distant buildings.

Looming.

But they were much too large.

One of them, it seemed, reached right into the heavens.

Finally, shakily, I stood up, and the little girl helped me.

"What's that?" I wondered, pointing at the huge building.

"That's the Anderson Building."

"It's way too big. Why doesn't it fall down?"

She smiled.

"It's only fifty-five stories."

Then she looked at me with a little girl's insatiable curiosity and wondered rather childishly:

"Are you from another planet?"

"It feels like it."

Then I heard something whirling above us, and I looked up into the skies, and I saw a strange metallic craft slowly gliding above the park.

Everything seemed too overwhelming, "too much," so when I spotted a nearby bench, we stepped over, and I sat down.

With the little girl, my ever-solicitous companion, standing right in front of me.

Ready to help.

I looked into her lovely brown eyes.

"Where am I?"

"Central Park."

"Yes, but what's the date?"

"June something."

"Yes, but what's the year?"

"2005."

I was overwhelmed with a debilitating weakness, with a sweeping nausea, with an all-encompassing revulsion.

I knew that everything, all of this, had to be a dream of some kind, but it didn't feel like I was dreaming.

The unreality seemed perfectly real.

Too real.

The little girl seemed to sense my hopelessness.

My fears.

My defeatedness.

She took my hands in hers, gently, as if to comfort me.

"Don't worry. I'll take care of you. I promise."

And, oddly enough, I knew that she would.

<u>24. Leaping Frog Café</u>

Monday, June 22nd

Nikki, dressed in her uniform, was sitting at an isolated table, beneath an outside pergola within the Wildlife Center's café.

She wasn't alone.

There was a stupid little capuchin monkey sitting on her shoulder, busily eating a tiny ice cream cone. I use the word "stupid" not as some kind of higher-species criticism, but because the strawberry ice cream was dripping all over its weird little hands, and it didn't seem to care in the least.

Nikki, similarly, didn't seem to notice.

She was distracted.

Impervious.

It was obvious that she'd already finished her lunch, sitting by herself, lost in thought.

Most probably worry.

I walked up to her table, fully aware that she'd probably take the fifth, yet knowing that I still had to make the attempt.

"I know all about 1905."

She looked up, trying her best to pretend that she wasn't shocked. Then she shook her head dismissively.

"You don't know anything about anything."

The know-nothing (me) sat down at the table, right across from Nikki and her weirdo companion.

I proved her wrong.

"I also know that Alice lives in the park. That she's lived here for the past ten years. And that she thinks she's going back to 1905 on June 25th, which is three days from now."

Once again, she was completely astonished, and, once again, she did her best to conceal it.

"You sound like a crazy person."

She lacked conviction.

"I also know that's why you're sitting here all alone and worrying. Because you're afraid that you're about to lose your best friend."

This time she didn't deny it. She just sat there and said nothing.

"Look, Nikki, I don't want to lose her either."

More nothing.

"Don't you realize," I pointed out, "that that ridiculous-looking creature is dripping strawberry goo all over your shoulder?"

Which got her attention.

"Jojo! What do you think you're doing! Get off there!"

Meaning her shoulder.

As for Jojo, as if having heard the voice of Yahweh, he immediately jumped down from Nikki's shoulder to the empty chair beside her.

"You're such a stupid slob sometimes!" she reprimanded.

"Aren't they all?" I wondered, but she didn't bother to respond. Then she wrapped Jojo's leash around the back of the chair, cleaned off her jacket, then cleaned off his creepy little hands.

"You just sit there and behave yourself," she warned him.

She wasn't messing around, and Jojo knew it. He sat back in his chair and looked as chastened as a monkey can look chastened. Then he stared at me as if I was the most interesting person in the world.

It was a bit unsettling.

"Can't he stare at someone else?" I wondered.

"He can stare at anyone he wants. It's a free country."

Which seemed an odd thing to say since the

monkey had a collar around its neck, attached to a long leather leash.

"Besides," she continued, "maybe he's wondering why you're bothering me again."

Nikki was always a little toughie, but I liked her.

I'd also checked her out. Or, at least, Helen had done the checking for me. She was twenty-two years old, meaning that she was twelve when Alice "transported" ten years ago, which seemed the best word that I could come up with for jumping a hundred years through time.

Nikki's mom had died when she was a little girl, and she was still living in the same Lexington Avenue apartment, up near 97th, just three blocks from the park, in southwest Spanish Harlem. Living with her widower father, Carlos Cabrera, a hardworking construction guy, who apparently had been doting on his daughter and only child for the past twenty-two years.

A bright kid, with a love for animals, Nikki did so well at signature school that she got a full ride to Fordham as a zoology major, but she dropped out after her sophomore year to take a job at the CP Zoo. I suspect that she dropped out to have more time with Alice, believing that, after June 25th, 2015, three days from now, she'd never see her again.

"What do you want from me?"

She seemed worn-out by my presence.

"I want you to tell me where she is."

Which seemed simple enough.

"I can't. She told me not to, so that's the end of that."

I wasn't leaving, and she knew it.

"Look, Rick, if you really love her, you'll leave her alone."

She'd called me Rick, and then she'd also used the l-word, both of which seemed like some kind of progress.

"I'll find her, Nikki."

"I wouldn't be so sure. She's been in the park for ten years, and she's got secret hideaways all over the place. Some that I don't even know about."

She looked at me directly.

"No one knows this park better than Alice. No one."

"All right, then help me out, Nikki. Who knows, maybe I can figure this thing out? Maybe I can convince her to stay."

She was obviously torn, and she didn't like it.

"I just can't do it. She asked me not to."

It seemed to me that Nikki was ready-and-desperate to try anything, but she couldn't betray a promise to her best friend.

She was helpless.

Which I understood.

I stood up.

The monkey was still looking at me intently. As if it had devoured and fully-comprehended every single word that I'd said. I wondered if it might raise its hand and ask a question.

"What's your boyfriend know?"

"I don't have a boyfriend."

But she knew that I knew that she was just being a pain in the ass. So I waited patiently for the real answer, and I got it.

"Eddie doesn't know a thing."

"Maybe he should."

Nikki shrugged, as if she didn't know what to think anymore.

"Yeah, maybe he should," she admitted.

I felt sorry for her. I'd only known Alice for a few days, a few odd encounters, and I already felt that I couldn't live without her. But poor Nikki had known her for ten years. Ten years of hiding her in the park. Helping her. Protecting her. I suspected that Alice was not only her best friend and confidant, but that she was also the sister-that-she'd-never-had, and maybe even the mother-that-she'd-never-had.

I felt that I shouldn't leave without at least acknowledging my most attentive audience.

"You behave yourself, Jojo."

But there was no response, just more of his dumb monkey stare, so I started to leave. Then Nikki grabbed at my sleeve, and I looked down into her eyes, which were flush with crushingly-deep fears and sorrows.

She tried to be nice.

Maybe because she'd seen the same fears within my own eyes.

"I hope you find her, Rick. She's never had someone like you before. She's never even allowed herself to think about it before, and I keep believing that it's a good thing for all of us, and I keep hoping that it'll change things somehow. That maybe 'what we think will happen' won't really happen."

She wasn't finished.

"I can't imagine my life without her. It's impossible."

"Neither can I."

I looked off into the far distances of the park.

"Well, at least, I know she's in the park somewhere."

But Nikki was back to being Nikki again.

"Yeah, good luck with that, pal! It's only 843 acres!"

25. The Praying

Monday, June 22nd

You were coming after me.

Again.

I was praying that you wouldn't find me, and I was praying that you would find me, and I was praying that if I did go back, it wouldn't somehow destroy everything. Meaning the entire current timeline. With you and Nikki and Eddie. That it wouldn't somehow obliterate/terminate all of you, and absolutely everything else, which I realize might seem rather self-absorbed and solipsistic, but it was, nevertheless, always the unspoken fear lurking beneath all my other terrible fears, and the one that I'd never mentioned to Nikki. Never. Not once. Whom I prayed had never thought to wonder about it on her own.

Yes, what would happen if I go back?

What would happen to this world, this timeline, this here-and-now, which would surely, in some way, be altered, if not actually eliminated? Unless, maybe, possibly, our incomprehensible cosmos permits and tolerates multiple timelines?

Multiple realities?

I prayed for that as well, thinking of what I'd once read in one of Stephen Hawking's books:

> *A butterfly flapping its wings can cause rain in New York City's Central Park. The trouble is, it is not repeatable.*

I tried to push it, and all such terrifying thoughts, from my vertiginous mind, and I thought, once again, of Ernest Dowson. Thinking of that poor, terminally-sad poet, dying of consumption and alcohol in Sherard's little cottage in Catford, who'd once written, in "Nuns of Perpetual Adoration," aspiring, as always, after the unattainable:

> *These heed not time.*

Which I repeated over and over, trying as best I could to flush all the other darkishness from my cruciated mind:

These heed not time.
These heed not time.
These heed not time.
These heed not time. . . .

26. Wellington Research Center

Tuesday, June 23rd

Eddie, looking rather sharp in his ranger uniform, was waiting right where I'd told him to wait. In front of the Wellington Building on Fifth Avenue near 83rd. I got out of Eric's Midtown cruiser and walked over to Eddie.

Who was eager to help.

"Hey, detective! What can I do?"

"You want to be a cop, Eddie?"

Which backed him up a bit.

"Yeah, I guess so, someday."

"Then you've got to stop lying to cops."

Which definitely embarrassed him, and he looked away, down at the pavement, like a six-foot-four little kid.

"Look, Eddie, I know you've known Alice for a long time, and that you've been covering for her."

"I'm sorry, but she's my girlfriend's best friend."

"I know, Eddie, and I understand. Now do you think that you're ready to start acting like a cop?"

"Yes, sir."

"Good. Now don't say a word unless I ask you a question."

He understood.

"Not a word," he repeated.

"Good. And call me 'Rick.' We're both in love with two best friends, right?"

He was fine with that.

"Right."

We took the elevator upstairs to the top floor and the main office of the Wellington Foundation, eighteen stories up, where we spent about five minutes in a comfortable waiting room, where I browsed through the foundation's brochure, which was mostly a recapitulation of what I'd already learned on the web last night.

Then a young secretary came into the room, and she escorted us into Miss Wellington's elegant and rather old-fashioned penthouse office. At the moment, she was standing across the huge room at its massive picture window, looking down pensively at the entire deep-green stretch of Central Park which lay right beneath her. When she heard us enter, she turned around and came over to greet us.

Cordially.

"I appreciate your time," I said, "especially on short notice."

"I'm glad to," she said, "especially if you have information about the young woman who calls herself Alice Appleton."

She gestured to a comfortable couch.

"Please, detective, have a seat."

Which we did.

Then the old lady also took a seat, in a nearby chair, beneath a rather impressive oil painting of a pleasant-looking man in a dark suit."

I nodded at the painting.

"Is that's James Wellington?"

"Yes, my father. He died in 1960."

She seemed saddened by the thought.

"I've read that he won the Nobel prize."

"Yes. For medicine. He processed a new vaccine that inhibited certain strains of Typhoid. Of course, no one can ever be certain about such things, but it's been estimated that his discovery has saved over 300,000 lives in both Africa and South America."

Eddie was so impressed that he broke his vow of silence.

"Wow!"

I was impressed too.

"That's a lot of lives."

She nodded, appreciatively.

"And the foundation?" I wondered. "I see that it supports medical research, but it also has a subsidiary interest in Time Studies."

"That's correct. My father wasn't a physicist, but he knew quite a few of them, including Albert Einstein, and he had a lifelong interest in the many theories and paradoxes relating to both time and space."

"Like time travel?"

Eddie's overwhelming bafflement kept him silent, but Miss Wellington was visibly impressed.

"I see that you're a smart young man."

She reached over to her desk and hit a button on her phone.

"Jennifer, please ask Dr. Russell to come to my office."

She looked back at me.

"Tell me why," I prodded.

Gently.

She thought it over and decided to tell the truth.

At least, the "truth" as she knew it.

"Why not, detective? When I was a little girl, my father told me fascinating stories about time travel. And one of them was about him when he was a little boy, when he nearly drowned in Central Park."

"On June 25th, 1905."

Now she was extremely impressed.

"Quite right. When I was still a child, I naturally believed all of his stories, but when I got older, I assumed that they were clever fantasies, just enjoyable stories that a father might conjure and fabricate to entertain his little girl, to stimulate her imagination. But later, closer to his death, he told me that his own story was true, and that he wanted the foundation to allocate a portion of its funds to further study."

"Why did he think his near-drowning related to some kind of time travel?"

"He believed, oddly enough, that it was how he was rescued, although I've never fully understood it, even though I did exactly as he wished with the foundation."

I believed her.

"So you think the girl in the park is actually Alice Appleton, your father's cousin?"

This was a bit too much for Eddie.

"What?!"

Then he stunned himself back into silence as we both ignored him.

"I really don't know. Is she?"

There was a knock on the door and a pleasant-looking man somewhere in his mid-fifties entered the room. He was wearing a comfortable dark suit, and I knew exactly who he was.

Miss Wellington stood up.

"Come in, Alfred, this is the young detective I've told you about."

She turned to me, and I stood up as well.

"This is Dr. Alfred Russell. He's a physicist, and he's the director of our Time Studies Department."

We shook hands, then everyone sat down, except, of course, for Eddie who was already sitting down and still trying to fathom all the weirdo stuff he was hearing.

I didn't waste time.

"You think it's possible?"

The doctor looked confused, so Miss Wellington clarified.

"Time travel, Alfred."

He smiled, rather warily.

"Oh, I suppose I do. If I lived a thousand years ago, I might have dreamed that voices could be transmitted around the world, or maybe even images, or that a metal machine could fly from New York to Los Angeles in a few hours. But I'm stuck in the Twenty-First Century, and I find myself dreaming about time slips, and dimensional rifts, and black holes, and even parallel universes.

I repeated myself.

"So you think it's possible?"

He shrugged evasively, and the old lady smiled.

"Remember, detective, he's a scientist. They never like to commit themselves. About anything!"

The physicist smiled, and Miss Wellington turned back to me.

"What do you think, young man?"

I hesitated, not certain if I could trust her.

"Let's be perfectly clear, detective," she tried to reassure me, "I mean her no harm. Just the opposite, in fact. After all, she might even be related to me, as impossible as that sounds! All I want to do is meet her and help her. And help you too."

I decided to trust her.

"All right, I believe that she *is* Alice Appleton. And I believe that she was, somehow, inexplicably, transported here from 1905, and that she's lived in Central Park for the last ten years."

"Whoa!"

It was Eddie again.

Once again, everyone ignored him.

I turned to Dr. Russell.

"What do you think of that?"

"Well, to be honest, it sounds perfectly nuts to me, but I'd like to be wrong. More than anything, I'd like to be wrong. And more than anything else, I'd like to meet this young woman."

The old woman looked at me.

Hopefully.

"Can you arrange it?"

"Maybe, but I've got to find her first. And that's why I've come here today. You told me that you've been searching for her for two years, and I was hoping that you might have some ideas."

"Unfortunately, I don't. Unfortunately, I have *no* ideas whatsoever. The park rangers tell me that they see her from time to time, but that's it. I think they like her, and I think that they're trying to protect her. I also think that they're suspicious that if they help me, then those unpleasant people from Immigration will catch her and arrest her."

She looked at Eddie.

"Isn't that correct, young man?"

"Yes, Ma'am."

I also looked over at Eddie and put him on the spot.

"Do you have any idea where she is, Eddie? All I want to do is help her."

He shook his head.

"I have no idea. No one knows but Nikki."

"Who's Nikki?" the old woman wondered.

"My girlfriend. Well, my ex-girlfriend."

Which, of course, was the wrong and unhelpful

answer, so I explained.

"Nikki is Alice's best friend, but she won't tell me a thing."

Frustrated, I stood up, walked over to the huge floor-to-ceiling window and looked down into the lush-green park which stretched out beneath us, between the Metropolitan Museum of Art and the distant Museum of Natural History on CP West.

Then I realized that the old woman was standing right next to me, also staring down into the mysterious park below.

"Could I be personal?" she asked.

I had no idea what she meant.

"Of course."

"In my youth, many years ago, I was twice engaged, but for differing reasons I called them both off, and, to this day, I still regret the first of my foolish decisions. As a consequence, I've never had children, and, since I was an only child, I've never had brothers or sisters. If that young girl down there is my relative, I want to meet her, and take care of her, and help her. In any way I can."

I believed her.

"Do you believe me?"

"Yes."

Gently.

"So why are *you* chasing after her, detective?"

she asked.

"Because I'm in love with her."

"I thought so."

"She's down there somewhere," I said, stating the perfectly obvious. "Somewhere in the park."

"Yes, and it's terribly huge."

She said it as if she'd just become aware of the fact for the very first time.

Then Eddie chimed in from the couch, with a lot of concern in his voice.

"843 acres."

Well, maybe it is.

But I'm a cop.

"I'll find her," I said.

Trying to believe in myself.

27. The Weight Room

Tuesday, June 23nd

I suppose I should have been getting myself ready, but the truth was, I'd been getting myself ready for ten years.

I was already ready.

So what was I supposed to do with myself? What does someone do before she jumps back in time a hundred years?

(Or was it a hundred-and-ten years?)

I did two things:

(1) Think about you.

(2) Try not to think about you.

When Nikki said, "I want to go talk to that idiot (meaning Eddie), you want to come along?" I thought to myself, "Why not?" I've always enjoyed their peculiar synergy, their curious interactions, and I could still fulfill my primary objectives, listed above and below, which I could do pretty much anywhere.

(1) Think about you.
(2) Try not to think about you.

Rather cleverly, rather surreptitiously (since I knew you were out there somewhere, searching everywhere, snooping all around the park, searching for me, which was, I have to admit, quite a lovely feeling), we made our way over to the little gym room at the rangers' headquarters and found Eddie working-out in his damp gray sweats, sitting on a bench doing dumbbell curls.

Which I knew wouldn't be overlooked by his girlfriend.

"Well, well, look at what the dumbbell's doing."

Nikki was frustrated. She was fed up. She walked right up to the one she loved, and she stood in front of him, as if intentionally intimidating him. Which, to an outside observer, would have seemed preposterous since Eddie's about 6'4", maybe 220, and Nikki's a very petite, very trim 5'5", maybe 110, if she was lucky.

As Nikki took her domineering position in front of her sitting boyfriend, her pretty little head was only slightly higher than his.

I sat down on a nearby weight-bench and watched the show. I always loved these little confrontations because, regardless of whatever silliness they were up to at the moment, they always seemed so perfectly charming, so lovely, so loving, because everything they ever did was completely subsumed by their underlying/unconditional love. Even though they seemed perfectly unaware of it. How many times in the past had I wished with all my heart that I could have something like that in my own life? Something so deep and so intimate. Then suddenly you came along from nowhere, and I found myself submerged in love.

So, I sat there watching the Nikki-Eddie show, thinking, of course, of you, and, of course, trying not to.

"Have you been helping that cop?"

She seemed more curious than angry.

Then I noticed that two other rangers were also working-out in a far corner of the room. When they realized that Nikki was "back," that she was actually in the weight room, they silently retreated even further into their isolated corner.

Wanting no part of it.

But Eddie was a slightly different Eddie today.

He wiped the sweat dripping down his face, and

he dropped the heavy dumbbell on the ground with a thud, and he looked directly at his little Nikki. Somehow, he seemed to have more self-confidence than he usually did. More self-assurance. And I knew where he was getting it from.

From you, of course, my love, whom I was and wasn't thinking of.

"Not until today, Nikki."

It sounded almost, but not quite, defiant.

"What does that mean?"

"It means that I learned more about Alice in twenty minutes with Rick Kincaid than I have with you ever since the day we met. Over five years ago!"

When Eddie mentioned my name, he looked over politely and nodded. Then he picked up a small towel and dabbed at his face, never taking his eyes off his little firecracker, whose fuse had fizzled.

Eddie was clearly disappointed and hurt that he'd been left out of things, and I suppose he had every right to be hurt and disappointed. Even Nikki seemed to agree, but she wanted things to be perfectly clear.

So the blame wouldn't be misplaced.

"You're right, Eddie. But it wasn't Alice's fault, it was mine. It was my choice."

Which made things worse.

"Why?"

He was suddenly back to being a little boy again.

A sweet little boy.

"Because I didn't want to complicate things. You're a park ranger, Eddie, and a good one, and I didn't want to put you in an awkward situation."

He wasn't convinced.

"I think you didn't trust me."

Nikki didn't try to deny it.

"I'm sorry, Eddie. I was wrong. I'm sorry."

Which was probably a milestone of some kind because Nikki never-ever admitted that she was wrong.

Never.

Certainly not to Eddie.

"Yeah, you're exactly right, Nikki. You were wrong. Totally. As for that detective, as far as I can tell, he's crazy in love with Alice, and he just wants to help."

He looked over at me again.

"I know, Eddie," Nikki agreed, "but I can't help him."

Meaning that I wouldn't allow it, which probably made me the villain in the story, but they both seemed to understand.

"I know, Nikki, but that doesn't mean that I can't try to help him out."

Nikki was speechless.

Another milestone.

Eddie looked at his love.

"Is any of this stuff true? All this 1905 stuff?"

He glanced behind him at the other guys currently doing squats in the back corner, and he turned back to Nikki and whispered.

"All this time travel stuff?"

"Some of it, Eddie, but I don't know the whole story myself, and neither does Alice."

He seemed to believe her.

He reached out and took her hand.

Gently.

"Look, Nikki, I'd like to undo the break-up thing?"

When she smiled, he kept going.

"I love you, Nikki Cabrera, and I'm going to make something of myself. For you."

There was absolutely no equivocation, and Nikki liked it. Her wonderful father was always a hyper-affirmative "get it done" type of guy, and that was all that Nikki had ever found lacking in Eddie.

"I don't want him to lose his sweetness," she once told me, "but I'd like a lot more conviction. A lot more self-conviction. Is that asking too much?"

(Actually, Nikki had told me that many more times than just "once.")

Now in the rangers' gym, Nikki leaned over and

kissed Eddie on the forehead.

Which was intended to settle everything.

Then she turned around, looked at me, and started for the door.

I stood up to follow her, but Eddie wasn't quite done.

"So what about it, Nikki?"

He called it out loudly, and the guys in the corner of the room looked over and listened in.

"What?" Nikki said confusedly.

"Do you love me or what?"

We all waited, wondering what tough-guy little Nikki would say, especially in public, especially with people listening in.

"Yes, lunkhead. Of course, I do."

It was time to make our exit.

I'd sat there the entire time, silently watching as they bantered back-and-forth, with nothing but love underlying everything they said and did. I listened carefully, loving their love for each other, yet still consciously fulfilling my primary directives.

(1) Think about you.
(2) Try not to think about you.

28. Castle

Tuesday, June 23rd

The one-man hunt was underway.

In earnest.

Last night, with permission, I'd searched through the Arsenal, which was finished in 1851, a few years before Central Park was created, and long before the events of 1905.

Meaning that Alice, when she was a young girl, on her strolls through the park, would have seen the old fortress in her earlier time.

I'd also gotten permission to go through their documents room with Helen, where we carefully examined all the blueprints and construction diagrams, both new and old, for every single one of the park's various structures, including the bridges, tunnels, and underground drainage pipes. We even took a look at the "Greensward Plan," which was the original proposal for the overall design of the park, created by its architects, Frederick Law Olmsted and Calvert Vaux.

I used to think, rather foolishly, that I "knew" the park, and that I knew it quite well, but now I was learning about its interiors, its underneaths, its foundations, and all its nooks and crannies.

All its potential hiding places.

"It's like hide-and-go-seek," Helen said.

"It's more like following Alice down the rabbit hole," I said.

She laughed.

Which was good because we were there for over six hours.

"You think you're ready?" she finally asked.

"Yeah."

So I got up early this morning, *very* early, eager to "run down" the one I loved.

Moving gradually from south to north.

From CP South to 110th.

I began snooping near the Pond and the Hallett Nature Sanctuary, fully aware that dug-outs, lean-tos, and even tree forts could be cleverly hidden from both the park's employees and its 42-million annual visitors.

Then I checked out Wollman Skating Rink and the Dairy, which, these days, served as the park's main visitors' center, always full of tourists and kids, always buying maps, t-shirts, tour guides, etc., within the beautiful old Victorian Cottage which was once, back in Alice's day, a restful retreat for worn-out children and their worn-out parents.

Everywhere I went, I was given carte blanche.

There's nothing like an NYPD badge, and the park workers and staff gave me full access to anything I wanted to see.

Maybe I should have felt bad about misusing my badge for personal reasons, but I didn't care in the least.

Later, I walked over to the ballfields, which I thought I knew pretty well before last night, but I didn't. I even checked out the old Carousel, which originally came from Coney Island and was one of the country's largest merry-go-rounds, whirling gently with its steam-whistle calliope.

Was it really possible that Alice could have been living in some hide-away hovel within the foundations of a merry-go-round? It wasn't very likely, but I was leaving nothing to chance.

No stone unturned.

Next, I spent a good chunk of time at the zoo, pleased that Nikki wasn't there, but neither was Alice. Just snow monkeys, snow leopards, sea lions, a few grizzlies, red pandas, penguins, puffins, and a billion other squawking birds.

Then I wandered around Sheep Meadow, the Mall, and East Green, looking I'm sure like a man, maybe a deranged one, who'd lost something that he was unlikely to ever find again.

After checking out Tavern on the Green, I stopped at Strawberry Fields for a brown-bag lunch, a cold but yummy Reuben with chips and a coke.

I was, I have to admit, feeling a bit discouraged. After all, Nikki had warned me that Alice had numerous hiding places all over the park, and I hadn't found a single one.

Nothing.

Not one.

But the sandwich helped. Soon I was over at the Boathouse, where I'd once danced with you-know-who. Then I checked out the Lake, the lovely Bow Bridge, the Ladies Pavilion, and Balcony Bridge, where I'd first kissed you-know-who.

Then I rambled into the heart of the Ramble.

Which was, of course, an endless, thirty-six acres of nothing but wildness. Searching up and down its hills and embankments, standing on top of all of its high points, using my never-seeing-a-damned-thing binoculars, then forcing myself down through the thick and tangled bush and foliage, which seemed more like a jungle than a ramble.

For hours.

Finding nothing.

Not even a little tree fort, not even the remains of an abandoned tree fort.

Nothing.

At 4:00, I came back to Trefoil Arch to meet with the locksmith. We immediately went into the drainage tunnel and wound our way underground to the metal grating.

Where he cut off the lock.

When we pushed the grating aside, I flashed my little cell-light and stepped within a damp, muddy, rather forbidding, three-foot-high passageway.

"I think I'll wait out here."

I couldn't blame the old guy.

After all, what would make anybody bend down and head into a dark dank claustrophobic tunnel?

Like Alice Appleton had done three days ago.

I continued inside alone, winding around endlessly beneath the surface of the park, making a few awkward slips and turns, occasionally hearing-and-sensing the vibrations of a road above me, which I assumed was Terrace Drive. Finally, after yet another sharp bend in the tunnel, I came upon another grating.

Seemingly terminal.

But this one, fortunately, was unlocked.

I pushed it open, and it screeched loudly, and someone screamed. When I stepped forward into the daylight, it took a few seconds for my eyes to adjust to the light.

Then I recognized where I was.

The Wisteria Pergola near Rumsey Playfield, and I'd just scared the hell out of some young girl, maybe fifteen, who was sitting beneath the pergola with her boyfriend.

Probably making out.

"Sorry about that, kids."

I shut the screeching grate behind me, then walked, this time, across the surface of the park back to Trefoil Arch, where I paid the baffled locksmith and sent him home.

By now, the sunlight was fading, so I rushed north to Great Lawn, trying to prevent my hopes from fading away as well.

Eventually, I climbed to the top of Summit Rock and looked at the entire park, scanning Cedar Hill, the Delacorte Theatre, Turtle Pond, the old bridle Path, and the Reservoir. Then I walked over near 84th to check out the foundations of the Met before I cut back to the Swedish Cottage and the Marionette Theater, where the kids would come in the late afternoons to watch the herky-jerky puppets act out *Peter Pan* and *Cinderella.*

Maybe even *Alice in Wonderland.*

Who knows?

I guess it was around eight o'clock when I made it to Harlem Meer and checked out Lasker Pool.

Completely worn-out, I crossed 110th Street, found a deli that was still open, and got myself another sandwich with some potato salad.

I think it was ham-and-cheese.

I can't even remember.

I was discouraged.

Yet I was also faintly hopeful.

Which I realize sounds contradictory.

I'd spent the entire day searching for something, anything, and I'd come up with nothing.

But I'd saved the best for last.

The castle.

Because late last night, standing with Helen in the Arsenal, as we were examining the old blueprints, we noticed something very interesting.

"Do you see that?" Helen asked.

"Yeah, I see it."

"Maybe it's something."

"Maybe it is."

But I had to save it for last because you can't search the Ramble and the Meadow in the dark of the night, but you can enter Belvedere Castle and search for a couple of never-used, shut-off old rooms in its lower basement.

Hoping to find someone inside.

Besides, wouldn't it be perfectly appropriate to find Alice Appleton hiding in a castle?

I headed south.

The old Belvedere Castle (yes, there really is a castle in Central Park) was designed back in 1865 as a Victorian fantasy castle. For years, it served as a national weather station, as well as the Henry Luce Nature Observatory. But like every other old castle, even ones that weren't that old, Belvedere had tons of secret hideaway rooms and closets. Including the one that Helen and I had spotted last night in one of the revised 2002 blueprints archived at the Armory.

Early this morning, Eddie had given me the key to the castle, so I had little trouble getting inside and making my way, with my cell-light, downstairs, through its complicated maze of rooms to a large and seldom-used storage closet full of old tech stuff and weather equipment. Carefully, I maneuvered my way through all the junk, slid one of the huge storage shelves out of the way and found the hidden doorway, which, unsurprisingly, was locked with a newish key-lock. Nearby, I found an extinguished old fire extinguisher, lifted it up over my head, and smashed the lock off its hinge.

With a tremendous crash.

Which would have woken up the dead.

I dropped the extinguisher, shoved the door open, and stepped inside the sealed-off room.

"Who's that?"

It was Alice's voice.

A bit groggy, a bit concerned, yet not-at-all terrified.

I flashed the little beam of my cell across the room at the head of her bed. She was sitting upright, holding the covers up to her neck.

Protectively.

"It's Rick. Who else were you expecting?"

I shut the door behind me, found a table lamp, and lit up the room.

Which I assumed was Alice's primary secret lodging within the park.

The room was small, sparse, but comfortably decorated, and completely windowless. Its large bed took up most of the room. It was old-fashioned, frilly, and girlishly attractive.

Her comforter was red.

The girl sitting in her bed and holding her comforter was beautiful.

I smiled.

"I've found you, Alice."

I guess I was proud of myself.

As for Alice, she seemed almost relieved, which

was also a relief.

"I wondered if you would."

She thought it over a moment.

"But why, Rick? What do you want from me?"

"Everything, Alice. Starting with the truth."

Which seemed simple enough.

She sat up even further at the head of her bed, resting back against the wooden headboard, surrounded within a dozen fluffy pillows.

Like a princess.

She was wearing a soft flannel nightgown, which was white and old-fashioned, and I knew exactly what kind.

Lanz.

Since she was still deciding how to respond, if at all, I tried to push her along.

"I know what happened in 1905, Alice. Over near Hernshead. With little Jimmy Wellington."

I handed her the old newspaper photograph. The one that Helen had found. The one with young Alice in her frilly dress, standing and smiling with her two younger sisters, each dressed in their own frilly dresses.

I guess I gave it to her as some kind of "evidence" to prove that I really did know, at least something, about her previous life.

She looked at it and went soft.

"Don't cry," I said. Worried.

"All right," she agreed.

I pulled a little straight-back chair over, probably Nikki's chair, and sat right next to Alice, right next to her bed, and waited.

She was remembering, and she told me about it.

"I couldn't swim back then, Rick, and I had no idea how deep the water was."

She seemed as if in a trance, in a dream, in another world.

Which she was.

"I was desperate, and I didn't know what to do."

"Well, you must have done something, Alice. Jimmy survived. Are you aware of that?"

She was stunned.

"That's impossible!"

"It's not impossible, Alice. You must have somehow gotten him to shore. Jimmy went on to become a famous scientist, and he saved many lives. Many lives."

She was having trouble believing it.

I held up my cell phone.

"I'll show you his wiki entry."

She shook her head.

"No, Rick. I've spent ten years avoiding anything that happened from 1905 to the present."

"Because you think you're going back?"

"Yes."

"Because you don't want to know what will happen after you get back?"

"Yes."

Which made sense.

If any of this could be said to make sense.

"Tell me what happened at Hernshead."

"I can't really remember, and I certainly don't understand how either one of us could have survived. I was terrified, Rick, and I was desperate, and I jumped. Then there was nothing. Nothing but blackness until I heard Nikki's voice, and I woke up, and I saw her, and her cell phone, and the huge Anderson Building, and a helicopter."

It was hard to imagine.

What if, for example, I was suddenly blasted into 2115?

It was hard to imagine.

"You jumped a hundred years."

"Yes. Isn't that perfectly ridiculous?" she said, still baffled by it all. "And little Nikki was kneeling over me. Like a little angel. Wanting to protect me."

"What do you think happened, Alice?"

"I don't know. Sometimes I think I drowned that day, and this is all a dream."

"I'm no dream, Alice."

She smiled, then continued.

"But maybe the worst part has been that I've had absolutely no idea *why* it happened. In time, I came to believe, and I still do, that there was some kind of purpose to all of it. Some kind of reason for everything that's happened. That maybe, most probably, I was supposed to go back in time and make things right."

"Save Jimmy?"

"Yes. So I've taught myself to become a strong swimmer. Very strong. And I've learned everything about emergency resuscitation, volunteering with the park's medical unit for over seven years. I've also worked hard to prepare myself mentally and psychologically, and now that you've told me about little Jimmy, maybe it really does make some sense."

"Does it? It seems that you've already saved him."

"But only if I go back and do it."

"Which makes no sense."

"I know, Rick, but you seem to believe that you're sitting here talking to a girl born in 1888, which also makes no sense."

She was certainly right about that.

Unsure what to say or what to do, I took her hand in mine, and she let me.

"How did you survive?" I tried.

"Nikki, of course!"

She smiled at the memories. Ten years of memories.

"She was a very resourceful little girl, even at twelve years old! She brought me food, and clothes, and she helped me build my first hideouts in the park. Then she convinced her father to get me a job with the gardening crew. A job I loved. The truth is, Rick, Nikki saved my life."

I waited for more.

"Her mom died when she was a little girl, and she's got no sisters and no brothers. So I became not only her best friend, but her sister, and I'm going to miss her terribly. I can't bear the thought!"

She looked into my eyes.

"And now there's you."

She was overcome with a deep-deep and sudden sadness, and I didn't know what to do, so I leaned over and kissed her on the forehead.

"You really believe you're going back in two days?"

"I do."

There was no hesitation.

"I have a strange feeling about it, Rick. It's hard to describe, actually it's impossible to describe, but it's like the whole world, or the whole cosmos, or something else that's terribly huge and inexplicable is telling me, deep within myself, that it's actually going to happen. On June 25th."

I believed her.

What else could I do?

"All right," I said, "then let's spend the rest of the time together."

She didn't resist.

"All right."

But that was it. She didn't make a move. She just sat there in her bed.

"So why don't you get up," I finally suggested, "and put on some clothes?"

She smiled.

"Why don't you go across the room and turn around?"

I laughed, and I did as I was told. Staring at a little wooden shelf with her few possessions: maybe ten books, a handful of DVDS, and a single CD, even though there was no TV in her room, or any other modern devices.

No cell, no radio, no computer, no I-pod.

The books were all histories, old ones, with one exception, *The Collected Poems of Ernest Dowson*.

Whoever he was.

I scanned the spines of the other books.

Burke's *Reflections on the Revolution in France* (which I'd actually read as an undergrad at Rutgers), Gibbon's *Decline and Fall of the Roman Empire*, several of the Greeks (Herodotus and Thucydides), and several books about the Middle Ages. It occurred to me that she probably didn't even know who Richard Nixon was, or Roosevelt, or Reagan.

Did she even know that we'd landed on the moon?

Did she know that there'd been two gargantuan devastating world wars?

How well had she been able to isolate herself from the future of her past life, which was, simultaneously, the past of her present life?

As for her DVDs, they weren't exactly strong on action-packed special-effects stuff.

Still not turning around, I kidded her about it.

"*In the Good Old Summertime, Life With Father*, and *Meet Me in St. Louis* – I'm seeing a bit of a theme."

"Yes, those are my three favorite movies, so Nikki bought them for me. Sometimes we watch them together, late at night in the Arsenal after everyone's gone home. They make me feel like I'm back where I've come from. Back home."

Then something dawned on me.

"Were you at the St. Louis World's Fair?"

"Yes. My father took the whole family! It was the first time I ever had an ice cream cone. Or cotton candy. And I still love them both!"

"What year was it?"

"1904."

The year before whatever happened happened.

"Are you decent yet?" I wondered.

"Yes."

I turned around.

I was still holding her only CD, which was marked, probably by Nikki, "Alice's Favorite (Stupid) Songs."

Once again, Alice was wearing another light summer dress, white with blue trim, with black Mary Janes, and a lovely smile.

"You look lovely."

She nodded down at the CD.

"I guess my tastes are a little bit out-of-date."

I checked out the CD cover and read off the first song title.

"'In the Shade of the Old Apple Tree'?"

"Yes, that's one of my favorites," she said happily. "So is 'Mary is a Grand Old Name' and Scott Joplin's 'Cascades,' which he wrote for the fair."

"People think my tastes are old-fashioned! The guys at 54th are always busting me about the Doo-Wop stuff."

Then, for the first time, I noticed a photograph on the little nightstand next to her bed, and I picked it up. It was a color shot of Alice and a very young Nikki smiling together somewhere in the park.

Maybe in the Ramble.

I was stunned.

"That's you and Nikki," I said stupidly, "and you haven't aged a day in the last ten years!"

"No, Rick, I haven't."

I put the photo back down, realizing that I'd never thought about her actual age before, always assuming that she was around twenty or twenty-one.

Something like that.

"How old are you?"

"I was seventeen in 1905, but nothing has changed."

"Nothing?"

She shrugged.

"Nothing, Rick. I'm still seventeen. I look exactly the same, and I've never been sick. Not once."

How do you respond to that?

Suddenly, there was a disturbing noise from outside her hidden doorway. Alice, quite naturally, was spooked, and she backed away. Instinctively, I pulled out my Glock, put a finger to my lips, and stepped closer to the doorway and waited.

Eventually, the door pushed in, and Dr. Russell entered the room.

Astonished, I lowered my weapon.

The doctor seemed oblivious.

"Is she here?" he said pleasantly.

When I turned around, the rest of the room was empty.

It was hard not to smile.

"I guess not."

Dr. Russell seemed concerned.

"I hope I didn't scare her away."

"No, I'm sure that busting into a young girl's bedroom in the middle of the night wouldn't scare anyone."

He seemed crestfallen, and I actually regretted my instinctive sarcasm.

Momentarily, at least.

Because, rather suddenly, there was even more noise loudly approaching from outside the doorway.

I glanced at the doctor with irritation, with anger.

"What's going on?"

"I have no idea. I was just sitting in the park earlier, and I saw you walk by, and I followed along."

I believed him.

Eventually, Murdock came into the room like he'd seen too many Eliot Ness movies, followed by two other blue-suited federal lackeys.

At least they hadn't pulled their weapons.

"Where is she?" Murdock demanded.

"Where's who?" I said.

He wasn't happy about it.

"You think this is funny, Kincaid?"

"Yeah, as a matter of fact, I do. A federal agent who can't find a seventeen-year-old girl! After two years!"

I was hoping, more than anything, that the schmuck would try to hit me, so I could bust him into a thousand pieces and burn off my considerable frustrations, but he seemed to recognize the fact that I shouldn't be messed with right now. He glanced over at his two clones, nodded, and they started snooping around the room, but, of course, there wasn't much to snoop.

Alice traveled light.

And lived light.

Murdock decided to start over, trying to be reasonable.

"Why's she living here in the park, detective?"

"Because she likes the fountain."

He was furious, of course, but he managed to maintain his self-control.

He looked over at Dr. Russell.

"Who the hell are you?"

I answered instead.

"He's my physicist."

Then I walked away, followed by my physicist,

who was, it was perfectly clear, enjoying himself immensely.

Murdock called out from behind me.

"I'm going to nail your ass to the wall, detective!"

I didn't care.

I was gone.

29. The Sneaking Away

Tuesday, June 23nd

How I hated to leave you again!

It was terrible.

But little Jimmy is waiting. Waiting somewhere in the far-off reaches and far-off recesses of an earlier time. Waiting to be saved, so that he can, in turn, save many others.

I snuck away, my love.

Once again.

Leaving you for the last time.

Which broke my heart. But I couldn't risk being caught, especially by that federal agent, the one that Nikki calls the "bully," along with various other choice descriptions.

So I snuck out through my ever-ready escape hatch, exiting the castle for the last time, sneaking over to my isolated bench within the Shakespeare

Garden, where I'd, so often, spent many wonderful hours tending to the primroses, the rues, the cowslips, the columbines, and I cried for a while. But I was tired of all my crying, fed-up with it, even though it was the only thing that seemed to make some sense. Maybe it was therapeutic. I hope so. Since I've met you, I've cried more than I've cried in the past ten years, and most of those years were extremely difficult and certainly worth crying about, but back in those days, I was focused, I was on a mission, and I still was until you came along and messed up everything. It was already hard enough leaving Nikki behind.

Now there was you.

Was I really supposed to go back to 1905 and allow myself to be courted and settle on some nice young man, who'd never know that I could never love him like I should?

Is that what I'm supposed to do?

So I cried.

Then cried some more.

Eventually, I snuck over to one of my little hovels in the Ramble. Aside from the Castle, and another secret room in the Arsenal, which I guess you hadn't figured out yet, I've always kept at least five other active in-and-out hideaways in the park that were always ready-and-waiting, which Nikki and I maintained and cleaned on a regular basis.

Because I never knew when I'd have to up and run, having almost-been-caught over a dozen times during the first eight years, and maybe another dozen or so during the past two years, ever since that "bully" ICE agent decided that I was not only an illegal alien, but a criminal as well.

After the Shakespeare Garden, I retreated to my very first hideaway, which was little more than a hovel in the ground, which Nikki and I created a few days after she found me in the park, half-drowned to death.

"You can't sleep outside all the time."

So she got a shovel from somewhere, and we dug a big hole in the thick dense middle of the Ramble, and we lined it with huge sheets of polyethylene which Nikki had lifted from one of her father's constructions sites, and we rigged up a pretty primitive yet well-concealed trapdoor.

In truth, it was nothing more than a dampish underground pit with an old thin mattress. Whenever the trapdoor came down over me, it was like being buried alive, buried underground, and I would lie there and think of my real bed and my real bedroom on Waverly Place, on the second floor of our lovely Greenwich Village brownstone home, where my grandfather had once lived next door to Henry

James' grandmother, facing Washington Square Park, close to the Washington Arch, and I'd wish and pray all night long that it was just a dream, a nightmare, and that I'd go back home, and that I'd wake up in my marvelous feather bed beneath one of my mother's marvelous quilts.

I pulled down the trapdoor, no longer feeling as claustrophobic as I used to, and I thought about the last ten years in the park, about my wonderful Nikki, and about you, and about the last five days. I also thought about the probability that, within two nights, on the night of June 25th, I would, most probably, be back at Waverly Place, sleeping in my own bed again, as if nothing unusual had happened, except of course for the rescue of Jimmy earlier that day, and I would lie there, awake all night in the darkness, perfectly comfortable, and long for you, as yet unborn, and maybe never even to be born, maybe never even to have existed at all, and crying myself back into the realities of my true existence, of my one and only one-and-true life.

<u>30. ICE</u>

Tuesday, June 23rd

I was sitting on a stone bench in front of the castle next to Dr. Russell, and I was sipping a coke. Not far away, there were two CP cruisers flashing their irritating red-and-blue lights, not far from the rangers' jeep and the feds' shiny black sedan.

Murdock and his two assistant pea-brains were still inside the castle, searching through Alice's secret bedroom looking for evidence.

Evidence of what?

A hundred-year transport through time?

"I shouldn't be enjoying this," Dr. Russell said.

Obviously, he was.

"Why not?" I said. "What the hell?"

If Alice was really going back on Thursday, then none of this mattered. But if she didn't go back, then I'd just blown her primary hideaway, and I wasn't happy about it.

I knew that Nikki wouldn't be happy about it either.

"Tell me more," the doctor asked.

"Why not?'

As you can see, I was in a "why not" kind of mood.

I told him pretty much everything that I knew about the mysteries of Alice Appleton, as he listened with a scientist's attentiveness and a child's absorption.

"It's curious," he decided, as if to himself, "that she believes that she came here from 1905, the year of Einstein's annus mirabilis, when he first published his special theory, and that her family drowned ten years later in 1915, the year he published his general theory of relativity."

"Does it mean anything?"

"Not really, but it's quite a coincidence! It's also around the same time that the idea of the 'leap second' started to be taken seriously."

He said it as if I should know what it was.

"What's that?"

"It was the realization that the division of the day into smaller units of time, which began with Ptolemy and led to our 'minutes' and 'seconds,' is a bit off, due to the sometimes erratic rotation of the earth. So a number of scientists proposed that a 'leap second' should be added every once in a while, to make things right. Just like we add the 29th of February in leap years, but they didn't start adding the leap second until 1972, even though it's still considered controversial in the scientific community."

"What's it got to do with Alice?"

"Nothing. Nothing at all. Just another curiosity."

"You're a big help."

He smiled, not minding my sarcasm.

Then he kept going.

"I've often wondered about the 'time' of time travel itself, assuming that it's really possible. If one could really transport, would it take up any time?"

"Like a leap second?"

"Yeah, something like that."

We were both, of course, just spinning our wheels, and we knew it, and it was oddly relaxing.

It didn't last for long.

Suddenly Nikki emerged from the darkness, looking like an angry Furia from Erebus, from deep within the Grecian underworld.

I wished that I could vanish like Alice.

Instantly, she was standing in front of me.

But there was more fear in her eyes than anger.

"Did they get her?"

"No, she slipped away."

"Thank God."

Relieved, physically drained, Nikki slumped down next to me on the bench. On the opposite side of the now silent physicist.

"How could you be so stupid, Rick?"

"I've got no answer for that."

"Try."

"I guess I was so focused on finding Alice that I never noticed that Murdock had a tail on me."

She nodded, as if understanding.

"It's no excuse," I offered.

She agreed, nodded again, then lightened up.

"You've been a great help, Rick!"

"Yeah, but if you told me where she was, then none of this would have happened."

Which was pretty lame.

"That's pretty lame, Rick."

"Yeah, I know."

"Don't worry, she'll be OK for tonight. She's got lots of other places where she can hide in the park. She's been ducking Murdock for two years, and we've never taken him lightly."

"That was my mistake."

Captain Palmer suddenly popped up from nowhere, heading toward me with Murdock.

He didn't seem particularly annoyed, and even Murdock was making an effort to behave himself.

"Rick, you need to answer some questions, and I've decided to referee."

"Fine."

Murdock began his inquisition.

"Do you . . . ?"

I cut him right off.

"No, Murdock, I don't know where she is. And if I did, I'd be with her right now."

"Why are you looking for her?"

"I'm in love with her."

Even the unflappable Murdock was taken back a bit.

So was the captain.

"How long have you known her?" he asked.

The fed was also confused.

"Five days."

Now the fed was irritated.

"That's ridiculous, Kincaid!"

"Yeah, that's exactly what she said when I told her that I loved her."

Nikki and the doc seemed to be enjoying themselves in silence, but Murdock got serious.

Fed-serious.

"Did she tell you that she was part of a check-kiting scam in Toronto that got a Mountie killed?"

I didn't know whether I should laugh in his face or punch him in the face, so I did nothing.

He tried to be reasonable.

"Look, detective, this is serious stuff. If you know where she is, you're harboring a fugitive. It's a chargeable offense. You could lose your badge."

"I appreciate your phony concern, Murdock, but I've already told you, I don't know where she is, and even if I did, I wouldn't tell you. So get off my back."

I guess the last part sounded like a threat, which it was, so the Ranger boss stepped in and put an end to everything.

"I think that's enough for now. It's perfectly obvious that Rick doesn't know where she is."

Murdock was smart enough to know it was true, so he nodded his agreement, and he and the captain walked back to all the police cars.

"He's the devil."

It was Nikki again.

"Toronto!" she scoffed, "She's never been anywhere in her life except for New York City! And St. Louis! And that was 1904!"

Nikki stood up.

The show was over, and she was ready to leave.

"I'm worn-out."

I knew better.

"You're going to see her right now."

It was both a statement and question.

"I think you've caused enough trouble tonight,

Rick."

She was right.

"Just tell her I need to see her again."

Nikki shrugged.

"Sure, why not?"

"Just one more time."

"Where?"

"Balcony Bridge."

"When?"

"2:00."

Since it was now past two in the morning, it was perfectly obvious that I meant later this afternoon.

"All right, Rick."

Then she put a comforting hand on my shoulder before she walked away.

I guess I'd won her over.

Finally.

We had a lot in common.

We were both about to be left behind.

31. The Longing

Tuesday, June 23nd

Maybe you'll die.

Maybe you'll no longer exist.

Maybe the whole present world will vanish because of me.

Nikki came in the middle of the night to make sure that I was OK and to tell me that she loved me.

She pulled up the trapdoor, and I got out of my polyethylene coffin, and we sat on the floor of the Ramble, and we held each other's hands.

She didn't want me to go.

She couldn't stand to lose me.

She couldn't bear it.

I said the same things to her.

Then, to push all the bad stuff out of our minds, we talked about some of our most fun-and-dangerous adventures over the past ten years. Like breaking into the Arsenal the first time; the day one of her stupid snow monkeys got out of the zoo and we had to chase it all over the park; the time we saved a young girl who'd crashed her bike and was bleeding to death near Greyshot Arch; the night we escaped from Murdock by climbing an old Elm tree not far from the Loch.

Stuff like that.

Lots of it.

Then Nikki told me that you wanted to see me again.

"Just one more time."

She told me where, and she told me when.

Then she left me alone because she said she needed to cry, and she didn't want me to see it, so I got back into my underground coffin, lay there alone in the darkness, in the midst of the world's greatest park, in the midst of the world's greatest city, and I thought about you.

Thinking, over and over:

"Just one more time."

"Just one more time."

"Just one more time."

32. Ladies Pavilion

Wednesday, June 24th

I was waiting on Balcony Bridge.

Again.

I was looking at the Lake and the park, so lovely in the summer sun, but, in truth, I really wasn't paying much attention.

Then I saw her.

She was sitting, not that far away, on the grassy shore of the Lake, wearing another white summer dress, looking as she always looked.

Beautiful.

Which is the word I keep overusing, right?

Maybe I should try "breathtaking"?

Yeah, I like that one a lot.

I quit the bridge, went down the bank, and came up behind her.

She was crying.

Maybe that was why she hadn't come up to the bridge. Maybe she wanted to get it over with.

I knelt down behind her, wrapped my arms around her, and she rested her head back against my chest.

Gently.

Then she tried to explain what didn't need any explanation.

"I'm sorry, Rick, it's just so hard."

Yes.

"I love my parents so much, and both of my little sisters, and I've missed them so much these past ten years. But I also love little Nikki, and now I've fallen in love with a city cop."

I didn't say, "I understand," because she knew it anyway. We stood up together, as she straightened out her dress.

Prim and proper.

Then we strolled over to Hernshead toward the secluded Ladies Pavilion, then up the bluestone path to the little open-air pavilion with all its intricate Victorian designs.

Inside, beneath its gray-slate roof, she stared at the Lake.

Thoughtfully.

"It happened right here," she remembered.

I didn't have to ask what *it* was.

"At Hernshead?" I asked, clarifying.

"Yes, up on those rocks."

I tried to picture it in my mind. The little boy falling, the little boy drowning, the young girl terrified.

She turned away and changed the subject.

"I used to skate here when I was a young girl."

"Were you any good?" I kidded.

"Yes, quite good, in fact."

I tried to imagine it.

"Back then, this pavilion wasn't here. It was over at 59th Street."

She turned, looking into my eyes.

"Why is this happening to me?"

Which was a question she didn't expect me to answer.

She corrected herself.

"Why is this happening to us?"

"I don't know, Alice, but just like you, I think it has some kind of purpose."

She nodded.

"Yes, little Jimmy."

"Was I right to tell you what happened?"

"Yes, it helps to know that I can save him. That I will save him."

"Was it hard," I wondered, "trying to avoid learning everything that happened afterwards? From

1905 to 2005? A hundred years of history?"

"Not really, Rick. I was curious, of course, but once I'd made up my mind, I never watched the news or read a newspaper, and Nikki and I picked our films very carefully. I've also never had, nor wanted, a cell phone. I guess I'm a bit old-fashioned."

She smiled.

"Just a bit," I kidded.

As she remembered:

"Ten years ago, just a few days after Nikki found me, after I'd finally accepted the fact that what had happened had really happened, Nikki brought her little laptop to the park, and when she turned it on, I was naturally tempted to look up my family, even myself, but I decided not to. Even back then, even in the earliest days, I always had the feeling that, someday, I'd be 'going back,' and if I did, I didn't want to know when my parents would die, or when I'd die, things like that. Or even what would happen in the world, like wars, elections, and other big stuff like that. So I avoided those hundred years as best I could."

"Did it work?"

"Pretty much, although I've learned a few things by accident, overhearing things that I didn't want to hear. I know, for example, that there was some kind of huge stock market crash, and that there was some kind of gigantic war, but I don't know any of the details, not even the dates. So I guess I'm ready to finally go back."

"That's why you didn't want me to tell you about the 1905 World Series."

She smiled.

"Yes, I'm a big Giants fan, Rick! As bizarre as it seems, I might be attending some pre-series games within the next few weeks."

It was hard to fathom.

As if from nowhere, there was salsa music, lively and incongruous, and Alice pulled out Nikki's cell, which, even without the music, was easily recognizable.

It's purple.

"It's Nikki."

Surprise, surprise.

She listened briefly, then responded into the phone:

"All right, Nikki, I'm coming. Right away."

She hung it up and put it away.

"I have to go."

I laughed.

"You two set that up! You took her phone and told her to call you. So you could get away from me."

She smiled one of her mischievous smiles.

"You're such a smarty-pants!"

She took my hands in hers and looked into my eyes.

"You have to let me go, Rick."

I didn't say a word.

"I'm afraid that you might try and prevent me tomorrow. That I might weaken."

She was getting emotional again, and I couldn't stand it.

"Please, Rick, you have to let me go! If nothing happens, I'll come and find you. I promise."

I believed her.

With all my heart.

"But you have to let me go," she repeated.

"All right," I said.

"Promise?"

"Promise."

"Have you ever broken a promise?"

"Not that I can remember, but I'd never break a promise to you."

When she was satisfied, I leaned forward and kissed her mouth, tenderly, lusciously, deliciously, lingering for a while.

Which she seemed to enjoy just as much as me.

"I'll keep away from here tomorrow, Alice. Far away from Hernshead at 2:00, and I'll let you go. I promise. But not until tomorrow. We still have tonight."

Whatever resolve she might have had when she was scheming with Nikki, with Nikki's cell phone, had now dissipated.

"All right, Rick. I'd like that more than anything, and I'm sure you can guess where I'll be tonight."

I was hoping for that.

"Yeah, St. Louis."

"I'll see you after the movie."

She turned, then walked away.

Into the soft Central Park summer sun.

33. The Dress

Wednesday, June 24th

I unzipped the garment bag and took out my dress.

It had been waiting in the back of Nikki's clothes closet, in her little bedroom on Lexington Avenue, for the past ten years. Two days ago, she got it dry-cleaned, and earlier this evening she'd brought it here, to the now-empty breakroom at the CP Zoo.

It was hard not to be emotional.

My mother had made me the dress for my sixteenth birthday in 1904. Since my father was a successful publisher, we could have, if we'd wanted to, purchased our dresses at the very best stores in the city, but my mother, despite her highly polished and gentile upbringing in London, was also an excellent seamstress, and her dresses were so much better than anyone else's dresses.

Besides, they were made with love.

Which you could feel when you wore them.

The birthday dress was what we called, back in the day, a "lingerie" dress, the meaning of which might seem a bit confusing in the current times. It was a white embroidered net, tucked and trimmed, with a collar-neckline, and it flowed down to the ground.

It was beautiful, and it fit me perfectly.

I remember crying when I first saw it on my birthday and hugging my mother so close, so tight.

I also remember when Christopher first saw it, when he smiled and said, "The only thing prettier than that dress is the girl wearing it."

I also remember wearing it on June 25th, 1905, standing at the Bethesda Fountain with my family, with all my cousins, when Jimmy, who was always my favorite (and didn't he know it!), tugged at the back of my dress, and I knew exactly what he wanted (to get away from everyone and play some kind of kids' game, probably hide-and-go-seek), and I said, "All right, Jimmy," and we walked away together towards Wagner Cove.

Towards Hernshead.

Towards the rocks.

"Here's your ridiculous hat."

Nikki was still struggling with the plastic

wrapping, and even I was surprised by the size of it.

I hadn't seen it in ten years since it had also been waiting in the back of Nikki's closet, hidden on a high shelf.

It was a lovely white Edwardian with a light blue ribbon and colorful flowers.

I stood in the breakroom and put on the dress. Then the hat. Then I looked at Nikki, who was sitting and waiting in her tight faded jeans and her bright red "La India" t-shirt.

Earlier this afternoon, she'd gone to one of the costume shops in the theater district for her own turn-of-the-century dress, as well as an appropriate suit for Eddie, and now her eyes got bigger and bigger and bigger.

"Wow!"

34. Meet Me in St. Louis

Wednesday, June 24th

I was standing at the north end of Sheep Meadow, leaning on a tree, dressed as I was usually dressed, behind all the mesmerized film-watchers spread out on their blankets on the lawn in front of the giant outdoor screen.

Which I was watching, just like the rest of them.

Watching the scene in the Smith family's snowy front yard:

Judy Garland (Esther Smith), wearing a lovely white overcoat, is crying in front of a tree, while her boyfriend, Tom Drake (John Truett), wearing a dark winter coat, stands nearby, rather helplessly. Concerned, but not knowing what to do, John offers Esther his handkerchief, and she takes it, and he apologizes.

"I wouldn't have said it, Esther, if I thought it

would make you cry."

"I've imagined you saying it thousands of times, and I always planned exactly how I'd act."

Judy smiles.

As only Judy can smile.

"I never planned to cry."

"Well," John says, still concerned, "at least you didn't laugh."

"Laugh?"

"I never asked a girl to marry me before. I guess I was kind of . . . "

"Oh, John! No one could have done it more beautifully. I'm very proud."

He seemed reassured.

Hopeful.

"Esther, will you? Will you, Esther?"

"Of course, I will, John."

Then they kiss, beautifully, holding each other closely.

"Gosh, the time we've wasted," Judy says (even pulling off the word "Gosh"). "Say, do you realize I might have lost you? Three more days, and you would have been gone."

Because Judy's old man was planning to move the family to New York City, much to the displeasure of the entire rest of his family.

"Let's not even think about it."

"We might never have seen each other again."

Which, I have to admit, hit home. With me.

How could it not?

"I kept telling myself that even if I did go away, we'd find some way to be together, but I never really believed it."

Yeah, Judy, I hope you're right about that, but I've got my doubts.

So I pulled myself "out" of the movie and scanned the crowd once again, looking for you-know-who. It was dark, of course, and everyone had their backs to me, many of them dressed in period turn-of-the-century clothing, imitating the film. When I couldn't find Alice (or Nikki or Eddie), I headed over toward the Bandshell area where I'd seen temporary concession stands selling, appropriately enough, cotton candy and ice cream cones.

I bought a large pink whirl of cotton candy and headed back to the screening. I was also carrying a small red rose and a bottle of red rosé in a little gift bag. Yeah, I knew that I shouldn't be carrying a bottle of wine in the park, opened or unopened, but what did I care?

I was a cop.

I was in love.

Look, I'd seen a few of those romantic movies over the years, those "rom-coms," and I knew that there was always a dance (which we'd already had at the Boathouse), and a kiss (more than one), and problems (let's not even go there), and a red rose, and a bottle of wine.

So I was doing my best.

When I got back to the meadow, *Meet Me in St. Louis* was wrapping up.

In the final scene, Esther is standing at a balustrade with John and the entire Smith family, all of whom are elaborately decked out for the opening day of the St. Louis World's Fair. None more so than Esther, who's wearing a spectacularly stunning frilly white dress, with a huge white bonnet and a matching parasol.

Fanfare is heard as the entire family, hearing the music, stops to look, and Esther is dazzled.

"Oh, look! The lights."

The family, in unison, looks out at the elegantly magical fairgrounds stretched out before them, as a million nightlights suddenly enflame, making everything seem like a child's elaborate playland.

Then, "Meet Me in St. Louis," the title tune, plays on the soundtrack.

"There's never been anything like it in the whole world!"

That's Esther's mother speaking.

Then Rose Smith, the oldest of the sisters, pipes

in.

"We don't have to come here on a train. Or stay in a hotel. It's right in our own hometown!"

Then it's little Tootie's turn.

"Grandpa, they'll never tear it down, will they?"

Grandpa reassures her.

"Well, they'd better not."

The film ends with a two-shot of Esther and John, both dazzled by the World's Fair.

Judy, of course, gets the final line.

"I can't believe it! Right here where we live! Right here in St. Louis!"

By the way, what is it about Judy Garland that you can't help but believe everything she says?

And who can crush your heart just by saying it?

As the final scene faded out, "THE END" appeared on the huge CP screen, and the final credits rolled. Gradually, the audience began to come back to the realities of 2015, applauding loudly, then standing up and discussing the film and admiring all the costumes. When the overhead beacon lights switched on, I scanned the crowd looking for my Judy Garland.

Holding her cotton candy and her red rose behind my back.

To surprise her.

Then I saw her in the crowd.

Coming toward me.

It seemed as though everyone in the audience opened up a path for her (which I'm sure was just my imagination), and she appeared to me like a vision, which I know is an easy cliché, but it's true. She wore a long white dress that made Judy's look like a backlot studio job, not to mention the hat, which was some kind of stupendous white bonnet.

I held out my rose, which seemed rather inadequate, and she smiled and took it in her hands.

She was wearing little white gloves.

Of course, she was.

"It's lovely, Rick. Thank you."

Then Nikki and Eddie popped up out of nowhere, still jabbering about the film, dressed in very attractive turn-of-the–century costumes.

I knew, of course, that Alice's dress was no costume, and I also knew that she'd be wearing it at 2:00 tomorrow afternoon on the rocks at Hernshead, but I pushed it from my mind.

"Should I tell you that you look beautiful, or are you getting tired of hearing it?"

"I never get tired of hearing it from you, Rick."

"You look beautiful."

She smiled again.

"And you look like you always look."

"How's that?"

"Handsome, casual, rough around the edges."

I laughed.

"Is that the dress you came in?"

Meaning 1905.

"Yes, Nikki's taken very good care of it. Just like she's taken very good care of me."

Nikki, never missing a trick, noticed something, and she stepped closer and smiled.

"You know the way to a woman's heart, copper."

Alice was confused, so I held out the cotton candy and watched her eyes light up like a child's.

So much for the red rose idea.

"Yummy!"

She carefully placed the red rose across the top of her purse and took the paper cone holder in her hand and looked at the wild whirl of pink sugar.

Which I once read is mostly air.

Which I once read is 99.999 per cent sugar.

(Which makes you wonder what the other .001 per cent is?)

Nikki laughed, happy to see her friend happy.

"Remember, Alice, we're meeting at the fountain at midnight."

"I'll be there. I promise."

Nikki looked at me.

"Take good care of her."

"I will."

Then Nikki and Eddie walked away, in the direction of the concession stand, and I had the feeling that Eddie was lusting for his own cotton candy.

"OK, so what's in the bag, Mr. Rough Edges?"

"A bottle of rosé."

"The days of wine and roses."

I had no idea what she was talking about.

"I've never actually had any, Rick."

"Wine?"

"Any kind of alcoholic beverage."

I suspected that there was only one person on planet earth who used the term "alcoholic beverage," and that there were probably only a handful of twenty-seven-year-olds (17 + 10) who'd never had a sip of wine."

"Maybe tonight's a good time for the first time?"

"Maybe."

But she didn't commit herself.

"So where's the most romantic place in the park?" I wondered.

She smiled.

"Well, that's easy! Balcony Bridge. Where you kissed me for the first time."

"Let's go."

So we did.

We headed over toward Hernshead, where we

both knew that everything might abruptly come to an end tomorrow afternoon, and, all the while, she carried her whirl of cotton candy, obviously saving it for later, probably already forgetting about the bottle of wine.

Then I asked her what I wasn't sure if I should.

She didn't seem to mind.

"Tell me about it."

She knew what I meant, but I made it even clearer.

"Tell me about your life back then."

"It was wonderful, Rick. Truly wonderful! We lived on Waverly Place, on 'The Row,' down on Washington Square. Do you know it?"

"Yeah, I know the current version. These days, NYU owns most of those historic townhouses."

"You went to school down there, didn't you?"

"Yes."

"A hundred years after I lived there."

Which still amazed the both of us.

"Tell me about it."

"Well, we weren't super-rich, but we were definitely privileged. Our home was lovely, we had a maid and a cook, and our lives were very comfortable. Teddy Roosevelt was president, New York City was endlessly exciting, and the New York Giants were the best baseball team in the entire world! I'd recently graduated from St. Anne's Academy, which I'd loved very much, and I spent a lot of my free time right here in the park. We had two horses stabled near 105th Street, and I rode the bridal paths at least once a week."

"Your dad was a book publisher, right?"

"Yes. My father and my grandfather and all my uncles. They published all kinds of wonderful books. Jules Verne, Sherlock Holmes, and, of course, *Alice in Wonderland*."

She smiled her mischievous smile.

"I was actually named after Alice Liddell, the original Alice."

I suppose I believed, at this point, that nothing could surprise me anymore, but I was wrong.

She explained:

"My mother was English, from London, and the Liddells were cousins."

"Tell me about them."

Meaning her parents.

She shrugged.

Which I suspect was something she'd picked up in the 21st Century. Probably from Nikki.

"I know it sounds terrible corny to say so, Rick, but they were just about perfect. All I ever wanted to do was grow up and be like my mother. I still do. And my father! He spoiled his 'three little girls' to death!

He loved to take us places like Dreamland and the brand-new Hippodrome, where we saw Harry Houdini!"

"Dreamland?"

"Yes, it was an amazing amusement park at Coney Island that opened in 1904. It had wild rides, exhibits, and, much like the World's Fair, spectacular lighting at night. Supposedly there were a million electric light bulbs that outlined all of the buildings in the darkness. It was spectacular."

When we got to Balcony Bridge, we sat down in one of the balconies.

"Tell me more," I said. "Tell me something special."

She smiled.

"Sure, how about Tanya?"

"Who's Tanya?"

"A horse."

She laughed.

"Tanya was a thoroughbred. A super-fast filly who won the Belmont Stakes on May 24th, 1905, beating out Blandy, who'd won the Withers, and her own half-brother Hot-Shot. It was terribly exciting, Rick, and I was right there in the stands with all of my family! A few years ago, Nikki told me that it took over a hundred years for another filly to win the Belmont. A horse named Rags to Riches in 2007."

"I thought you didn't want to know anything about those hundred years?"

I was kidding.

"I guess I made a few exceptions."

"Tell me more."

She fake-pouted.

"Then can I eat my treat?"

(Who uses the word "treat"?)

"Of course."

She stood up.

"Let's go to Hernshead."

Which meant the Ladies Pavilion, where we'd been earlier this afternoon.

"Sure."

I stood up, and we strolled down the path toward the Lake.

"All right," I prompted.

"All right, I've already told you about my trip to the World's Fair in St. Louis, but you probably didn't know that the Olympics was going on at the same time, and we got to see Archie Hahn, the world's fastest sprinter, known as the 'Milwaukee Meteor,' who set an Olympic record in the 200. We also saw him win the 100 meters and the 60 meters, which I guess they don't have anymore. It was truly amazing!"

It was, I have to admit, exciting to witness her own excitement. If I really had to lose Alice tomorrow, it was a small comfort, yet a real comfort nevertheless, to know that she was returning to such a comfortable enjoyable life.

Without me.

"So you're a big sports fan?"

"Yes," she reminded me, "I'm a huge Giant's fan."

"Did you go to many games?"

"Tons!"

"Which, I suppose, is where you met your boyfriend."

"*You're* my boyfriend."

"Is that what I am?"

"Oh, you're a lot more than that."

"Which I'm glad to hear, but you're avoiding the question."

"Yes, nosybody, I saw Christopher pitch six different times."

(Is "nosybody" a word?)

"Christopher?"

We were, of course, talking about Christy Mathewson, the "Big Six," one of the greatest pitchers of his time, or any time, who won 373 games, with 79 shutouts, and a 2.13 lifetime E.R.A., and, of course, even though I couldn't tell Alice about it, he was one of the first five elected into the Baseball Hall of Fame in 1936, along with Ruth, Johnson, Cobb, and

Wagner.

I also couldn't tell her that he'd be the superhero of the 1905 World Series, when John McGraw's Giants would beat Connie Mack's Athletics four games to one, with the Big Six winning three games.

Because she might, within the next few months in her own time, be going to some of those 1905 World Series games.

"Well, he wasn't born 'Christy,' you silly boy."

"Keep going."

"Fine, I'll admit, I did have a bit of a crush on him, if that's what you're snooping around for, but so did every other girl in New York City."

"But you actually met him, right?"

"Yes, after one of the games. After he'd pitched a two-hitter. Then he went to my father and asked him if he could escort me on a walk through the park."

"A date?"

"Yes, a date."

"How many times?"

"Once."

"Did he kiss you?"

She smiled.

"No, he was much too polite and respectful, unlike someone else I know."

I couldn't let it go.

"Did he want to see you again?"

"Of course, he did."

"Will you?"

"No."

Even though I was relieved, I felt like a fool.

"You know, Rick, jealousy isn't very attractive."

"I know, but I can't help it."

"Our one-and-only date was about a month before I came here. Christopher was taking off on a road trip with the team, and he'd pitched a no-hitter against Chicago twelve days before I jumped into the 21st Century. I was supposed to see him again when he got back to New York City. But I won't."

A moment ago I felt like a fool, now I felt like a jerk.

When we arrived at the Ladies Pavilion, she looked out at the Lake.

Her destiny.

She turned and looked into my eyes.

"Maybe you should also know, Rick, that I'd also had three marriage proposals earlier that summer, but you don't have to worry about it, Mr. Detective, I've fallen in love with somebody else, and nothing will ever change that. Nothing."

She held my hand, and I was feeling quite ashamed of myself, and she knew it.

"Kiss me," she said.

So I did.

She wiped away the past.

She wiped away the future.

At least momentarily.

Then she looked deeply into my eyes.

"Can I finally eat my cotton candy?"

She was smiling again.

"Yeah, sure, gobble up your 'treat.'"

She wasn't insulted in the least. She immediately stuck out her tongue, as ladylike as possible, and touched it against the spun pinkness and its sugar ecstasy.

Unaware, apparently, that the tip of her nose had also made contact with the pinkness.

I didn't say a word.

She sat down on one of the wooden benches and finished what she'd started, eating the entire super-sticky thing, as I sat next to her and watched her and wished that I could watch her forever.

When she finished, she looked down at her little white gloves, which were still, miraculously, perfectly white, and she seemed quite pleased with herself, unaware of all the congealed splotches of sugared pinkness on her face.

"You're a mess," I said.

"Am I?"

She seemed genuinely surprised, but not embarrassed.

"It's all over your lips."

"Kiss it off, tough guy."

I did.

Kissing my love in the moonlight.

"I bet that tasted yummy."

"Nothing is yummier than you, with or without the sugar."

She liked that a lot.

"All gone?" she wondered.

"Not by a long shot."

I took out a wet nap, opened it up, and wiped her face.

She was amused.

"You certainly come prepared."

"I'm a cop."

Then I took her pink-stained paper cone, stood up, and dropped it, along with her pink-stained wet-nap into the garbage can. When I sat back down, I got serious.

I was prepared.

"Alice, there's something you need to know about your future back then. It's important, and I think I need to tell you about it."

Which clearly violated Alice's policy of assiduously avoiding her 1905-plus future.

"I trust you, Rick."

So, I told her.

"On June 25th, 1915, your entire family will be on a boat in the Hudson River celebrating the wedding of one of your younger sisters, then the boat will capsize, and everyone will drown."

She was stunned.

"Everyone?"

"Yes, but now that you know, you can save them."

Should I have also told her that she'd already, in the current timeline, drowned ten years earlier on June 25th, 1905? (Which, of course, made no sense.) That she'd somehow been able to save her little cousin, but that she'd drowned herself in the process? At least, according to all the newspaper accounts that Helen had been able to track down.

Maybe I should have.

But I didn't.

She'd been preparing herself for ten years. Nikki told me that she could swim like an Olympic swimmer. If she really did go back tomorrow, I had no doubt that she'd rescue little Jimmy, save herself, and then, ten years later, save her entire family as well.

"There *really* is a purpose to all of this, Rick."

"Yes."

"More than one."

"Yes."

She was still processing everything.

"It's another June 25th."

"Yes, exactly ten years later."

She shook her head.

It was incomprehensible.

She didn't even bother to say "How strange" or "How bizarre" because everything was already so strange and bizarre.

She stood up again and looked at the Lake.

I stood up as well, hearing a distant chime from across the water.

"It's quarter to twelve, Rick. I have to go."

She was sad again.

"Like Cinderella," I said.

She smiled.

"Yes, like Cinderella."

She turned to me, took my hands in hers, and told me what every man on the planet wants to hear from the woman he loves.

"I love you, Rick. More than I could ever say or explain. With a depth that crushes my heart."

But there was more.

The downside.

"But I want you to do exactly what you promised this afternoon. I want you to stay away tomorrow. I need to be strong, Rick, and I'm afraid that I'll falter if I see you again."

I understood.

"I will."

"There are too many lives at stake."

"I know."

She was almost crying again, which I didn't want to see.

"Will you promise me again?"

"I promise, Alice. But if things don't work out the way we think they will tomorrow, if you're still here at 2:15 tomorrow afternoon, floating around in the Lake in your beautiful dress, looking like some kind of crazy person, can we make a life for ourselves right here in the 21st Century?"

"I'll still be trapped in the park."

"It's a big park."

She smiled.

"Look, Alice, I don't care about anything else. We'll get married here in the park, and I'll take care of the feds, and we'll work everything out. Everything."

"As strange as it sounds, it's exactly what I want to do, Rick. More than anything! I want to be here with you."

She fell into my arms, as I held the world in my embrace.

"Why must love be so difficult?" she whispered.

I had no answer.

I kissed her again.

"Don't move! Either one of you!"

It was loudish, boorish, self-important, and the worst case of bad timing in the history of the world.

It was, of course, Murdock, and I wasn't pleased.

Not a bit.

He walked up to the pavilion, followed, as usual, by his two ICE clones, and I stepped in front of Alice.

"Get the hell out of here, Murdock! You have no idea what you're doing."

I was angry. Naturally. Which he perceived as a threat, so he pulled his service weapon.

"I don't want any trouble from you, Kincaid."

I wasn't the only one who was angry.

When Murdock stepped into the small pavilion, getting too damned close, I smashed his face in. Sometimes when you hit a guy, it's a bit off-center, a bit off the sweet spot, a bit off-the-mark, but not this time. Murdock dropped like a bag of bricks, blacked out unconscious, and his gun went flying.

Fortunately, his two subordinates were stunned into motionlessness, so I pulled my Glock before they could make a move to help their boss, who lay inert on the wooden floor of the pavilion.

I stopped them in their tracks.

"Don't think I won't use this."

When they saw my Glock in the moonlight, they took me seriously.

Of course, all I really wanted to do was get Alice

out of there, but when I turned around to look for her, she was already gone, probably halfway to the Bethesda Fountain to meet with Nikki.

For their final night together.

It was hard not to laugh, but I had an image to project.

"Drop your weapons."

They did as they were told.

"Now I want you to walk down to the Lake, walk into the water, and I don't want you to turn around until it's up to your chest."

They didn't like the idea.

I lifted my piece again.

Which always gets people's attention.

"Now!"

They started walking down toward the water, and I followed after them.

At the water's edge, I reassured them.

"Your boss'll be fine. Now get in the water."

Which they did, fully knowing that as soon as they got into the Lake, chest-high, they'd turn around, and I'd be gone.

I never went home that night, of course, spending most of the night up on the roof of the old Dakota, where John Lennon once lived, where I could sit in the blackness, in the faint moonlight, and look down into the park, so eerily beautiful, so dark and mysterious.

Where I could eat my little Smarties in solitude.

Ten small rolls of biconcave candy discs.

Fifteen in a roll.

Where I could think about Alice, and think about Alice, and think about Alice, and think about how stupendously screwed-up my life was.

35. The Rock

Wednesday, June 24th

I was sitting on Vista Rock again.

Writing these sorry pages, being a rather shoddy account that I've written just for you, written in the rush of the past two nights, of which I'm not very proud.

But I wanted to leave you something behind. I wanted to leave something (beside the book) that might in some inadequate way show you just how much you mean to me, how much my absurdist life has been shattered by your extraordinary presence.

How much I love you.

Once again, of course, I'd had to run away last night. As it was approaching midnight. Leaving you behind with those nasty federal agents. So naturally I'm very worried about you. Surely, there'll be consequences for doing what you did, even though I know that, somehow, you'll "deal with it," to use one of Nikki's favorite expressions.

I met Nikki a few minutes after midnight at the fountain, and we went off to the familiar solitude of the Shakespeare Garden, amid the primroses and columbines, and we tried to "deal" with the impossibility of losing each other. Normally, Nikki never cries, at least not in front of anyone, even me, but she cried a lot earlier tonight, and we held each other, and we stayed up until around three a.m. or so, and then she went home. We would have liked to stay up the entire night, alone together, but we knew that I'd need some sleep for tomorrow, if sleep was a possibility, given that I had to save a little boy from drowning tomorrow afternoon.

Nikki hugged me, left for home, and I came up here, high above the park, and wondered where you might be, knowing that you were thinking of me, the one who loves you more than all the world itself.

Thinking of a line in one of Dowson's poems, wishing it could, somehow, be true for us, for me, for you, whom I'll never see again.

Never.

But droop into my arms and understand!

36. Miss Wellington

Thursday, June 25th

Eddie, dressed in his ranger uniform, was standing, once again, in front of the Wellington Building.

When I got there, I didn't waste any time.

"You got it, Eddie?"

"Yeah."

He handed me the file.

"Summarize it."

"Well, for starters, Murdock's 'Alice' was born in Quebec City, and she's thirty-five years old."

He handed me a photo of a pretty worn-out dirty blonde.

"That's just one of her mug shots. One of the better ones. She's doing time in some kind of women's detention center in Ottawa."

"Murdock's an idiot," I said, stating the perfectly

obvious, handing both the photo and the file back to Eddie.

"Good work."

Which he clearly appreciated.

Eddie was ready to help me in any way possible, even if it would get him into trouble. It was easy to see why Alice liked him so much, and why Nikki loved him so much. I felt certain that when everything was over, we'd be friends, and that I'd do everything I could to get him a spot in the Academy.

"Let's go upstairs."

"Sure. What's up, Rick?"

"Let's find out."

On the 18th floor, we were escorted, once again, into Miss Wellington's office, and she was standing exactly where she was standing the last time we'd arrived, staring out her huge picture window at the park below.

"Come in," she said.

She turned around.

She seemed glad to see us, but a little bit concerned.

"Are you in trouble, detective? I've heard there's a warrant out for your arrest."

Eddie was astonished.

I hadn't told him about my little get-together with Murdock last night at Hernshead.

"I'm fine," I lied, "but there's something I didn't tell you about Alice."

She was naturally intrigued, so she gestured to the couch, and we sat down in the exact same places as the last time.

I told her.

"Alice believes that she's going back today. At 2:00. It'll be exactly ten years from when she first came here, on June 25th, 2005."

The old woman was amazed and naturally skeptical.

"Do you believe it?"

"I do. But, of course, I can't know for sure. I've been thinking about it all night long, and there's just too many things that don't make sense."

"Is there anything I can do?"

"Yes, that's why I'm here. I'd like you to tell me exactly what your father told you when you were a little girl. Everything."

"Of course. I'll try. I'll do my best."

"Everything," I repeated, needlessly.

"My father was six years old at the time, and he readily admitted that he was always full of boyish energy and mischief. He particularly looked forward to Sunday afternoons, when he was allowed to go to the park with his cousins, the Appletons. He was completely enamored of Alice Appleton, the oldest of the three daughters in the family, who was, I believe he said, about seventeen years old at the time, and who was also, as he told it, remarkably beautiful."

She hesitated a moment.

"Just like your Alice. Just like the one I spoke to after her lecture in the Shakespeare Garden."

Once again, Miss Wellington focused, thinking back deep into her past.

"My father told me that Alice had always treated him like he was her favorite little cousin, and Sunday was his absolute favorite day of the week. Sometime, in the heat of the summer in 1905, maybe in June, they all went to the park, and my father waited patiently for a chance to get Alice all for himself. Finally, near the Bethesda Fountain, he tugged on her dress, and she smiled, and she agreed to take him for a walk, just the two of them."

The old woman smiled at the memory of her father's memory.

"Of course, Alice knew exactly what he really wanted, and, as they were strolling along through the park, he got her to agree, as she always did, to play a game of hide-and-seek. Then he ran off ahead of her, trying to find a special hiding place that would really impress her. Eventually, over near Hernshead, he foolishly climbed out on a high limb over the Lake, which was especially foolish since he couldn't swim."

She stopped.

"Apparently, very few people knew how to swim back in those days. Not even sailors."

Which was something I'd also heard.

She returned back to 1905.

"Anyway, when Alice arrived at the Cove, he waved to her from his branch, but he lost his balance, and he fell into the water. He managed to make it back to the surface, gasping for air, and he even saw Alice standing above him on a rocky promontory. Even though he was just a little boy, he knew exactly what was happening. He was drowning. He was terrified. All of a sudden, Alice jumped into the water, but he never saw her again. Then, out of nowhere, the traveler dived into the water and saved his life."

"The traveler?"

"Of course, the time-traveler. That's what my father's story was all about. The traveler suddenly appeared from nowhere, and he rescued my father."

It was hard to say who was more stunned, me or Eddie.

"*He*?" I asked. "A male?"

"Of course. Poor Alice had tried to save him, but she ended up drowned, and my father was haunted by that terrible memory for the rest of his life."

"Do you know his name?"

"The rescuer? Yes, of course, but only his first

name. He insisted on absolutely no publicity, and the family respected his wishes. Which is why he was never mentioned in the newspaper accounts."

I tried to be patient.

"What was his name?"

I already knew the answer.

"Richard."

"That's my name."

I said it rather anticlimactically.

Instantly, I knew what I had to do, and so did Eddie, and so did Miss Wellington. I checked my watch and stood up, ready to leave.

"I have to go."

She understood, and she stood up as well.

"You're going back?"

"I have to try."

Unexpectedly, she took hold of the sleeve of my windbreaker.

Gently.

"If you do go back, tell me about it."

Which didn't make any sense.

"How?"

"Write an account and leave it in the New York Public library. Leave it in the Appleton file, and Eddie can pick it up later today."

We were all amazed by the possibility.

"Please, it's all I'll have. Tell me everything."

"All right, I will. Everything that's happened in the past eight days."

Since she needed further assurance, I gave it to her.

"I promise."

"Thank you, Rick."

I nodded.

Then Eddie and I headed for the door, but she called out behind us.

"Eddie! You come back here tonight and tell me what's happened. One way or another."

"Yes, ma'am. I promise."

<u>37. The Lake</u>

Thursday, June 25th

It's noon, and I'm finishing up these pages.

My brief "account."

I don't know what else I should call it.

Just a few more sentences.

A few more poorly written fragmentary sentences, reflecting, I guess, my state of mind.

Nikki'll be here soon, and we'll go over to the breakroom at the zoo, and I'll put on my dress again. Then around 1:40 or so, we'll walk over to the Lake. Hopefully, my clothes won't attract too much attention.

Just a few curious looks.

After all, it's New York City.

Then Nikki and I will try to say goodbye.

But I'll do my best to stay focused, stay determined. I'll hand her these handwritten pages, along with the book, and I'll tell her to give them to you. I'll also tell her that I'll write a letter "just for her," from the distant past, and leave it at the New York Public Library.

In the Appleton Collection.

Then I'll tell her how much I love her.

Then I'll stand at the edge of the precipice, and when I should be thinking about nothing but saving little Jimmy, and saving my whole family, and saving all those poor people with Typhoid, I'll be thinking of nothing but you.

Which I've been doing all day long.

Which I've been doing ever since I saw you across CP West with a bullet through your leg.

Ever since we looked into each other's eyes at Umpire Rock.

Then I'll leap into a world without you.

Which will seem like a totally meaningless world, but not one without love.

Because I'll love you until I die, long before you're even born.

Forever!

38. Great Lawn

Thursday, June 25th

In the Wellington elevator, I wrote a check for Eddie, which covered my entire bank account.

Roughly $215,000.

"This is for you and Nikki."

What else was I going to do with it?

"And here's the key to my place. Everything is yours, Eddie. Including the baseball statues. Everything."

He was hesitant.

"I'm not sure I believe any of this stuff, Rick."

"Then it's just-in-case, Eddie. Just-in-case."

Meaning, oddly enough, if I don't really vanish.

Vanish into nothingness.

At least, from this timeline.

But poor Eddie was still stuck within his incomprehensions.

"This can't be happening, Rick."

I put the check and the key in his hand, and he looked down, rather stupidly, at the check.

"That's over two hundred thousand dollars!"

"Look at me, Eddie."

He did.

"Tell Michelle that she can stay there as long as she wants and give her $30,000."

"Michelle?"

I had no time to unbaffle his bafflements.

"Whenever she's out, the place is yours. There's nine months left on the lease. Then I want you to find Helen at Midtown and tell her that I love her and that I already miss her."

"Helen?"

"Yes, then tell her the truth. The *whole* truth."

Eddie shrugged.

What else could he do?

My cell phone rang out a Doo-Wop tune.

"Could This Be Magic."

Naturally.

But I was still focused on Eddie.

"Listen to me, Eddie, there's nothing wrong with being a ranger, but if you really want to be a cop, then you just need to do it. I'm sure you can pass the stupid test. I'm positive."

He didn't respond.

"Are you hearing me, Eddie?"

"Yes."

"Will you do it?"

"Yes."

I glanced down at my cell phone and read the text.

"Damn it! Baaden's over in the park!"

Immediately, Eddie snapped out of it.

"The guy who shot you?"

"Yeah."

I thought things over.

Quickly.

"Of course!" I said to myself out loud. "Every loose end needs to be tied up."

I checked my watch. It was 1:15.

"We can still make it."

I looked at Eddie.

"You want to bust a punk?"

"Yeah!"

He was excited.

We exited the Wellington Building, crossed Fifth, took the path along the north side of the Metropolitan Museum of Art and headed for the Great Lawn and the soccer fields.

Helen was right. Baaden would never miss the mid-summer tournament.

Over the past few days, my leg had been

recouping nicely, and I was doing just fine.

Ready to run if necessary.

When we spotted Baaden on field #6, I made my way over to the tree line, behind all the spectators, so Eddie could flush him out. Even from a distance, it was obvious that Baden, dressed in his team-blue shorts and team-blue t-shirt, was a highly-skilled forward, supposedly one of the best in the park, and I watched him maneuver closer and closer to the goal, ready to strike, when he looked up and saw Eddie standing in front of the net, looking very much an intimidating 6'4".

Baaden was spooked, but only momentarily. Rather deftly, he kicked the ball up to his hands, tucked it under his left arm, and started running in the only direction that made any sense.

Toward the tree line.

Where I was now lurking behind a stand of young pines.

As Baaden got closer, quickly outdistancing Eddie, I stepped into his path, and I pulled my Glock.

Thinking how nice it would be to plug the slimy punk before I took off on my little excursion.

As for Baaden, he stopped, pretty much on a dime, and looked at me, knowing exactly who I was.

He was considering his options.

Meaning which way he should run next,

obviously assuming that I'd never really shoot him.

But I wasn't in the mood for wasting any more time, so I blew a 9-mm right through the soccer ball he was still holding beneath his left arm, and the punctured ball immediately went "whoosh," as the now-released captive air suddenly rushed out into the summer sunshine.

Baaden, who was always cocky and fearless, was visibly shaken.

"Why not run for it?" I tempted him.

He was afraid, uncertain what to do.

Which was good.

"Look, Baaden, I'll be glad to blow a hole through your leg."

It was clear that he believed me, and he resigned himself. Suddenly, Eddie swarmed all over him from behind, drove him hard into the dirt, and then, rather quickly and professionally, cuffed the creep's hands behind his back.

But time was running out.

"Good job, Eddie. Call it in, and they can read him his rights when they get here."

But Eddie, who was now kneeling over the prostrate Baaden, looked at me like I was crazy.

"No way, Rick! Hell no! I'm not missing anything! I'm going to Hernshead!"

I guess I couldn't blame him.

Eddie stood up, as Baaden, still on the ground, squirmed himself into a sitting position.

"What about him?" I asked.

Eddie shrugged and looked around.

"I'll cuff him to one of those benches over there."

I didn't like the idea, so I stepped closer to Baaden.

"Hey, you!"

He looked up, and I smashed him in the face with a very hard right, and his stupid head slumped to the side, and he fell over unconscious.

"That's for Michelle," I said, even though the bastard couldn't hear me.

Or anything else.

I turned back to Eddie.

"All right. Pull him over to the benches and lock him down."

I checked my watch.

It was 1:46.

"I've got to run, Eddie! You can catch up later."

I ran.

And ran.

Past Turtle Pond, along the northwest edge of the Ramble, over Balcony Bridge, toward Hernshead.

I suppose that my leg might have been hurting at the time, but I didn't notice.

Then I saw her up ahead, at the edge of the rocks.

But she wasn't alone.

39. Aftermath

Thursday, June 25th

[Additional note by Nicolasa Cabrera.]

Alice, dressed in her dress, stood at the edge of the precipice.

Earlier, we'd done our heart-to-heart.

Lots of it.

Sitting in the same spot where she was now standing, with our legs dangling over the edge of the small promontory.

Over the Lake.

Alice was wearing her lovely 1905 dress, and I was wearing my zoo uniform.

Hey, what does one wear to say goodbye forever to one's best friend?

Oddly enough, I'd thought about it a lot. I wondered if I should wear the same black t-shirt I was wearing ten years ago when I pulled her from the Lake. The one my dad once bought me because he thought it was "cute."

So did I.

The one that said: "IF LOST RETURN TO THE CENTRAL PARK ZOO."

Which I still had in my closet in a little plastic bag, never wanting to lose it, never wanting to lose anything that was important or significant relating to Alice, to our very first meeting, being the most important thing that had ever happened to me in my life.

But in the end, I decided against it.

I was "on the clock" at the Zoo today, even though my zoo-pals were covering for me, and I thought it was more appropriate to say goodbye in my little uniform, which I loved so much, and which Alice loved so much, and which, of all the clothes that she'd seen me wear during the past ten years, it was what she always liked the most.

By far.

With loose beige-pants tucked into my high dark boots, with a buttoned-up and collared beige blouse, with "ANIMAL DEPT" on the right breast, with "WILDLIFE CONSERVATORY SOCIETY" on the left.

It was, I figured, how she'd probably remember

me.

So we sat there together, above the cove, which was (fortunately) deserted and beautiful as always.

Naturally, I was depressed and sad and distressed.

"I can't stand it!" I said.

Or something like that.

Just like a child.

Alice put her arm around me, as she'd done so many many times in the park and gave me comfort.

"Neither can I, Nikki, but we have to be strong."

To be honest, I wasn't consoled by her "strong" idea, so I shrugged in frustration.

So she tried another approach.

"I'm going to leave you a letter in the New York Public Library. It'll be in the 'Appleton Collection.'"

It seemed preposterous, so I didn't say a word.

"Please, Nikki, just find it and read it."

"I will. I promise."

"Which you can do later this afternoon."

Which was beyond preposterous.

"This is nuts!"

I hugged her close to me again, very close, and she reminisced.

"Do you remember when you were twelve years old, and you told me that someday you'd be the director of the zoo?"

"Yeah, I was a pretty cocky kid."

"You were my angel. My guardian angel."

Which always made me go soft.

"Don't let whatever happens today hold you back, Nikki. I need to believe, more than anything, that you'll still do exactly what you've always wanted to do, run the zoo, take care of the animals, and make life wonderful for all the little kids in the park. Will you do that, Nikki?"

"Yes."

If that's what she wanted, then that's what I was going to do with the rest of my life.

Nothing would get in my way.

"Can I give you some more advice?"

I laughed.

It felt odd to laugh, but I did.

"Sure, nothing's ever stopped you before."

She smiled, and I assured her.

"And I've always listened."

Which was true.

"In the past, I've always avoided this subject, but I think you should say 'yes' and marry the guy. Eddie's the sweetest guy in the whole world, and he worships the ground you walk on, and I know that he still makes your heart thump. Am I right?"

I couldn't deny it.

"Yeah. I don't have the foggiest idea why he does, but you're right, he does. All right, Alice, if it'll make you happy, I'll marry the big idiot!"

"Only if it'll make *you* happy."

"It will, Alice. You're right. Anything else?"

"Yes, please be kind to Rick. Check on him from time to time and make sure that he's OK."

"I will."

"You can tell him how much I love him because no one knows better than you."

"I will."

She checked her watch. The little Timex I'd bought her in some hockshop ten years ago.

My heart sank.

It was time.

She stood up, and so did I.

We hugged for the last time, and she kissed me on the forehead.

Then she took off her watch and handed it to me.

I guess it wasn't 1905-appropriate.

"I'm ready, Nikki. I'm ready to do what I wasn't able to do a hundred-and-ten years ago."

She was definitely ready. Even if I wasn't. I've never known anyone more determined to do what she thought she had to do than Alice. And I loved her for it.

She looked into my eyes, which I assume were mushy-wet and dripping.

"Pray for me."

It was the last thing she ever said to me.

"I will."

I meant it.

Then I backed away to watch the unwatchable.

"Stop, right there!"

I knew the voice, of course. I'd know it anywhere. It was that moron Murdock, trying once again to muck things up. I turned around and saw him approaching with his two younger agents, and I was fully ready to throw myself at his feet and try to trip him. After all, he was twice my size. I was ready to do *anything* to keep him away from Alice.

Meaning, I hate to admit, that I was fully ready to bite the bastard.

No one likes to get bit, not even federal agents, and that would definitely slow him down.

As for Alice, she didn't even turn around. She seemed perfectly calm. In another zone. Which made Murdock even more furious, so he pulled out his stupid gun.

"You better not jump!" he yelled, and I almost felt sorry for the guy. By all accounts, he was a decent agent and generally kind to all the dispossessed he had to pick up for deportation, but Alice had gotten under his skin. How many times in the past two years had she slipped away from him and easily escaped?

Way too many times not to damage both his pride

and his reputation.

Nevertheless, I didn't feel that sorry for him, and I was fully ready to throw myself in his path, gun or no gun, and try to buy Alice the few more seconds she needed.

The chime went off.

I'd never noticed it before.

Alice jumped.

We could hear the splash below us.

Then from nowhere, someone (was it Rick?!) came racing toward the promontory, intentionally smashing into Murdock and knocking him to the ground, as he rushed past all of us.

I heard the second chime.

It was two o'clock.

I watched in amazement as Rick ran right to the edge of the rocks and dove into the water below.

Another splash.

Then I saw that Eddie was coming too, and I was greatly relieved.

Still in shock, all of us (me, Eddie, and the two younger agents) walked over to the edge of the precipice and looked down into the water.

Nothing.

No one.

Not a single ripple on the serene surface of the Lake.

No one said a word.

Eventually, Murdock got up and made his way over to the edge and looked down just like the rest of us.

At the slick calm surface of the Lake.

"Where the hell are they?"

He seemed more amazed that angry, and his two agents didn't even bother to respond.

After all, what could they say?

Murdock looked at me.

"Where are they?"

I shrugged.

"You wouldn't believe me if I told you. No one would."

"Try me."

"They just jumped a hundred-and-ten years into the past."

He didn't believe it, of course, but he also didn't give me a hard time about it.

Maybe he wanted to believe it.

Later, sitting on the edge of the precipice, Eddie and I gave our statements to one of the younger feds. We really didn't have much to say, and he didn't press us too hard.

When he left, I held Eddie tight.

"What just happened?" I wondered.

It was clear that Eddie knew a lot more than

either Alice or I would have expected.

"I think I've got some idea," he admitted.

"Are they together?"

"I think so. Let's go find out."

We stood up, hand in hand, and went to the big library on Fifth.

I was still holding Alice's present for Rick.

Obviously, a book.

I was still holding Alice's pages for Rick.

Which I assumed was some kind of testament.

A testament of love.

Which, I guess, he'll never get to read.

40. 1905

Sunday, June 25th

I surfaced.

Looking for Alice, but I saw the little boy instead. He was flailing and failing and gasping and drowning, so I came up behind him, put my arm around his small chest, and swam him to shore.

I pulled him onto the bank, where he lay on his back, awake and coughing, but I knew he'd be all right.

But what about Alice?

Where was she?

I stood up and looked out at the Lake and saw nothing.

It felt as though time was running out.

Another fear ripped through me. What if I'd come all the way back, but Alice hadn't? What if I was stuck here in the past, so that I could save this little boy, and Alice was still swimming around in the Lake with Nikki and Murdock watching from the rocks?

I scrambled on top of a nearby bench, dripping wet in the hot June sun, staring intently at the surface of the Lake.

Then I saw, not Alice, but her white dress, floating ever-so-gently, undulating lightly, just beneath the surface of the water.

She was face down.

Which was terrifying.

I dove in again, swam out to the whiteness, grabbed her just as I'd grabbed little Jimmy, around the chest, and swam her, with some difficulty, back to shore.

"Pulled" her to shore would have been more accurate.

She felt like dead weight, like a thousand pounds, and I was constantly impeded by the swirling whirls of her long white dress, ever-tangling around my arms and my legs.

But I made it.

I pulled her onto the shore, where Jimmy, now recouped and nervously aware of what was going on, was waiting. He was also, I'm sure, anxiously aware that everything was his fault, and he was probably silently praying for his favorite cousin, who now lay lifeless on the grassy bank.

Breathless.

Looking as though she was dead.

But there still was a pulse at her neck.

Faint.

I didn't have time to allow my mind to think about it, or worry about it. Or become fearful. Immediately, I knelt over Alice, pushed the wet hair from her face, and started CPR.

Mouth-to-mouth.

"What are you doing!"

The little boy was obviously horrified, having no idea what I was doing, and it must have seemed rather creepy, rather ugly.

I ignored him, of course, and I did exactly what I'd been trained to do at the Academy, and which I'd done a half-dozen times on the streets of New York City as a Midtown cop.

She didn't respond.

She seemed too far gone. Dead.

"Don't leave me, Alice!"

Then I was immediately back at it again.

Counting, working feverishly.

I remembered the time, over near 58th and Ninth Avenue, when I was the first at the scene after a little girl, maybe ten or twelve years old, had fallen off a fire escape, and I bent over her prostrate form, with blood all over the place, and I pressured the wound at the top of her head, while, at the same time, doing my best mouth-to-mouth, trying not to panic, trying to do it exactly as I'd been taught, exactly as it had worked several other times, and I just kept going and going, even though it was pointless, until my sergeant finally arrived, and told me to stop.

I stopped eventually, knelt upright, and looked down into the dead girl's eyes.

Which were open.

Alice's were closed.

"Stop that!"

I guess Jimmy thought that I was hurting her somehow, or maybe smothering her, and he didn't like it.

"What are you doing?!"

I ignored him, and, exactly like that time on 58th, I tried not to panic. I tried not to think. I continued working on Alice for much-too-long, without any response whatsoever, knowing that it was perfectly useless, when I felt the little boy grab at the back of my still-soaked windbreaker, which I'd been too stupid to remove, and pull me off her.

Gently.

I knelt up straight and looked down at the one I loved.

She looked perfectly beautiful, even soaked, pale, dead, and unrevivable.

Had I really come back a hundred years just to lose her?

Was everything about the little boy?

Saving the little boy?

Saving the little boy who would eventually save so many others?

"Kiss her."

It was the little boy.

Who'd probably read too many fairy tales.

Who'd probably read them with his pretty cousin, Alice.

"Kiss her," he insisted. "Like a lover."

Maybe he was right.

Mouth-to-mouth didn't count.

So, I bent over and kissed my lovely Alice, gently on her soft cold lips.

I know this sounds perfectly ridiculous, but let's face it, it's no more ridiculous than all the other ridiculousnesses that had been going on in our lives.

Her lips were wet. She tasted like Alice.

Wonderful.

She stirred.

She squirmed a bit, just like some princess waking up from a long nap. Then she opened her eyes and looked at me.

"See! That's how it's done!"

Jimmy was obviously pleased with himself, but Alice was still dazed and confused.

"Are you all right?" I asked rather stupidly.

"What happened?"

She remembered, and she was terrified.

"Where's Jimmy!?"

Jimmy stepped closer so she could see him standing above her, and all was suddenly right with the world.

With Alice's world.

"I'm right here, Alice!" Jimmy assured her. "I'm fine. He saved me too!"

Alice, still lying on the bank, looked up at me again and tried to explain herself.

"I'm sorry. I don't know how to swim."

I laughed.

"Of course, you do. You can swim better than me."

Then it hit me.

I realized.

Was it possible?

"Don't you know me, Alice?"

She looked at me with appreciation.

But not with love.

"You're the one who just saved my life. Thank you."

Thank you?
All of this for a "thank you"?

41. Library

Thursday, June 25th

[Additional note by Nicolasa Cabrera.]

I was sitting on the stone steps of the New York Public Library, at the north end, close to the lion known as "Fortitude."

Which seemed appropriate.

In my lap, I had Alice's "memoir," the one she'd written for the now vanished Rick, as well as her present for Rick (which, no surprise, was her old copy of *Alice in Wonderland*, the one with the famous illustrations by Tenniel, now inscribed, "To Richard, to the one and only love of my life"), and I'd just finished reading Alice's note for me, which was quite short, extremely bizarre, unsettling and disturbing, and I was crying.

Earlier, when Eddie and I found the archive

room, the elderly archivist told us that "it might take a while" so we sat down at an isolated table, and I opened up Alice's "memoir" for Rick, and we read it together in silence.

It was perfectly lovely.

It was Alice.

Exactly.

So loving, so lovely.

Eventually, the archivist reappeared with an oldish flattish box marked, "APPLETON." Inside, there was a manuscript from Rick for "Miss Theresa Wellington, Edward Mendosa, and Nikki Cabrera," along with a thin letter for "Miss Nicolasa Cabrera."

Which, right-off-the-bat, struck me as peculiar.

Both the "Miss" and the "Nicolasa."

"Can we keep this stuff?" Eddie asked.

"Of course, I've seen your IDs, and according to the instructions, it's yours to keep."

Although I'm sure she was naturally curious, the librarian didn't intrude, and she left us alone at the table.

I stared down at the letter.

I was apprehensive.

I'm not sure why.

Eddie, who often seems to know me better than I know myself, knew that I needed to be alone.

"Look, Nikki, why don't you stay here and read

your letter by yourself. I'd like to read over Rick's account and then check-up on a few things."

Alice was right.

He was the nicest guy in the world.

"Why don't we meet outside," I suggested, "at one of the lions in about thirty minutes or so?"

"Which one?"

"Fortitude."

We both knew that the letter would take just a few minutes to read, but I wanted to read it over and over again, so I could think about it over and over again.

"Good."

Eddie stood up, bent down, kissed me, and wandered off into the maze of the great NYC library. Then I stood up, made my way outside, and sat in the soft afternoon city-sun, reading the letter from my now long-dead best friend, which began:

> *My dearest Nicolasa: I suspect that you're reading this letter on June 25th, 2015, which is, of course, hard to comprehend. I hope you're sitting comfortably in the Library Archives, or, maybe, outside on the library steps near one of the lions.*

By now, I'd read it a dozen times, and I still

didn't know how I should feel. It was certainly not at all what I'd expected.

"You OK?"

It was Eddie.

He could tell, of course, that I wasn't OK, so he sat down beside me.

"It's hard, Eddie. *Very* hard."

He understood.

"So what," I wondered, "have you been doing?"

"Reading Rick's account and doing some snooping. It's pretty amazing, Nikki. He goes all the way back to 1905, saves them both, and then Alice doesn't even remember who he is."

Which was reaffirmed in my letter from Alice.

"But eventually, in the end," Eddie continued enthusiastically, "it all worked out all right. She fell in love with him all over again, a second time, and they got married, and they had four kids. So, everything turned out all right."

I wasn't so sure.

When I shrugged, Eddie tried again.

"He told her everything that happened, Nikki. About you, about Central Park, and she believed him. All of it."

"I know, Eddie."

Eddie could tell that Alice's letter had bothered me quite a bit, and he was kind enough not to ask me about it, which I appreciated.

"When did Rick write it?" I wondered.

"July 7th, 1905. One week after they both reappeared in 1905."

Eddie looked at me.

"When did Alice write your letter?"

"Ten years later, which was a week after the boating disaster was prevented."

"I guess he saved the whole family," Eddie said, as if to himself, in amazement.

"Yes."

We sat there in silence for a while, and I was very grateful for the silence.

Eventually, Eddie spoke again.

Gently.

"I've done some checking in the library, Nikki. About their lives after 1905. Do you want to know the rest of it? How it all turned out?"

I didn't.

"Not now, Eddie. I realize that they're both long dead, and I'd rather not think about it right now."

He kissed me on the cheek, and I liked it.

Which gave me a chance to change the subject.

"You know what Alice said before she left? She said that I should say 'yes' to my boyfriend."

"Well, it's about time! I'm always ready to get down on my knee. What'll it be, Nikki? The sixth time?"

I smiled, but he didn't get down on his knee.

"What's up, Eddie? Second thoughts?"

He smiled his Eddie smile.

"I only propose in the park."

Despite everything, I laughed.

"Yeah, you're right, Eddie. Let's go to the park."

So, we stood up together, in the heart of the greatest city in the world, and he took my hand in his.

"Yeah, let's go to the park!"

<u>42. Letter</u>

Thursday, June 25th

I was now somebody's "fiancée."

Later that afternoon, when we got back to the park, we went over to Hernshead, and Eddie got down on his knee for the sixth time, and I said 'yes.'"

It felt right.

It felt wonderful.

Then alone and together, we read over Rick's account of the past eight days, me for the first time, and Eddie for the second.

Which ended:

> *I loved her in the 21st Century. Then, after that, I loved her in the 20th Century. 100 years apart.*

It was a love story, a lovely story, and I loved it.

Yet it seemed somehow incomplete, somehow unresolved. Maybe because they were now long-dead and long-forgotten, even though, just this morning, they were here in the park, alive and well in 2015.

"That shouldn't be the end of it, Eddie."

He didn't disagree, and I thought about it some more.

"Maybe we could combine Rick's account with Alice's account? Maybe we could even publish it? Even if it's just for you and me."

"And our children."

I liked the idea.

Eddie had another idea.

"I bet Miss Wellington would help us out."

I liked that idea too.

We sat on one of the benches in the Ladies Pavilion, holding hands and trying to wrap our heads around everything, all the incomprehensibilities. Finally, as he'd promised, Eddie needed to go over to Fifth Avenue and meet with Miss Wellington.

"I think I'll stay here, Eddie."

He understood, kissed me on the forehead, and headed across the park.

So I wandered all alone toward the Shakespeare Garden, where I could re-read my letter, and think about Alice.

And try to "deal" with it.

My dearest Nicolasa:

I suspect that you're reading this letter on June 25th, 2015, which is, of course, hard to comprehend. I hope you're sitting comfortably in the Library Archives, or, possibly, outside on the library steps near one of the lions.

Many possible tragedies in my life have been prevented by Richard and his love for me. But the greatest and still-unresolved tragedy is that I have no memory of you, my dearest friend, my protector, my confidante, my sister, my love.

Richard has told me all about you, over and over, and I've struggled with my mind to try and remember you, to try and remember anything about the ten years we spent together in Central Park. If only I could remember your pretty face, which Richard has done his best to describe. If only I could remember all the fun we must have had, and our many secrets and adventures and dangers. If only I could remember your kindness. If only I could remember the closeness between us. If only I could remember what Richard describes as your "cocksuredness," your "cockiness," words we don't use in 1915, and your mental and physical toughness, a word seldom used to describe women in these times, even though so many women really are "tough," especially when they have to face serious difficulties in their lives.

I hope you can forgive me, Nikki. I hope you can forgive that I have no memory of you. But I do have a mental portrait of what you must have been like, based on everything that Richard has told me.

I believe that you saved my life, and that you gave me hope, and that you gave me love.

It breaks my heart to write this letter, knowing it will be a disappointment, since it will lack the personal. But be assured that it is not lacking in either feeling or gratitude.

Or love.

As you read this, I will, of course, be long dead, but as I write this I'm very much alive with the hope and the prayers that your life with Edward will be blessed, and that you'll always know that I love you deeply, deeply, deeply, even though I'm unable to recall our times together.

With an admittedly odd but ever-true love and affection, Alice

I cried again.

Not just for myself, but for Alice, struggling so hard to write the "right thing" to someone, to me, off in her far far distant future whom she had absolutely no memory of, while still certain that, within her past, she'd loved me deeply.

And been loved the same.

43. Editor's Note:

The combined narratives, edited by Nicolasa Cabrera Mendosa and Edward Mendosa, with the assistance of Miss Theresa Wellington of the Wellington Foundation, was first published as a "novel" by Random House. It debuted on June 25th, 2017, appeared on the best-seller list the following week, and settled in for sixteen successive weeks at #1.

The movie rights are now in discussion.

A year after the book was published, Helen Rodgers of the Midtown North Precinct discovered, through genealogical research, a further inexplicable curiosity: that Alice Appleton Kincaid was actually the great-great-great-grandmother of Nicolasa Cabrera Mendosa.

A fact that we thought might be of interest to the reader.

William Baer is the award-winning author of more than thirty books including the Jack Colt mystery series *New Jersey Noir*, the Deirdre Flanagan mystery series, *Companion, Advocatus Diaboli, Times Square and Other Stories, Classic American Films*, and *One-and-Twenty Tales*. A graduate of Rutgers, NYU, South Carolina, the Johns Hopkins Writing Seminars, and USC Cinema, he's been the recipient of a Guggenheim Fellowship, a Fulbright (Portugal), an NEA fellowship in fiction, and the Jack Nicholson Screenwriting Award. He lives happily in a log cabin in the lake region of north New Jersey.

www.ingramcontent.com/pod-product-compliance
Lightning Source LLC
Chambersburg PA
CBHW070412310726
48977CB00003B/660